"Five days from now, with the rise of the Kissing Moon, nineteen of our best archers will use you for target practice."

The prince straightened his green waistcoat and glared anew at Rollo. "Since you're such a big target, we'll adjust the range. I trust your death will be swift, and that it will end this curse."

"There's no curse," muttered Rollo, slumping onto his haunches. "Killing me won't make your lives better. Bad things can still happen, even in the Bonny Woods."

The regal elf spread his fingers. "Five days, troll, until the moon is right. You will be fed better, but no more visitors. Make peace, or whatever you trolls do."

"Fine," muttered Rollo, picking the straw out of his toe talons. And then he began to plan his escape.

THE
TROLL QUEEN
JOHN VORNHOLT

Read all of the books in The Troll King trilogy:

The Troll King

The Troll Queen

The Troll Treasure

(Available soon)

From Aladdin Paperbacks

Published by Simon & Schuster

THE
TROLL QUEEN

JOHN VORNHOLT

ALADDIN PAPERBACKS
New York London Toronto Sydney Singapore

First Aladdin Paperbacks edition August 2003

Copyright © 2003 by John Vornholt

ALADDIN PAPERBACKS
An imprint of Simon & Schuster Children's Publishing Division
1230 Avenue of the Americas
New York, NY 10020

Designed by Debra Sfetsios
The text of this book was set in Times New Roman.

Printed in the United States of America
10 9 8 7 6 5 4 3 2 1

Library of Congress Control Number 2002115615

ISBN 0-689-85833-7

For Louis

CHAPTER 1

RETURN TO FUNGUS MEADOWS

"THERE'S LUDICRA!" WHISPERED A FEMALE TROLL AS A shapely mass of fur, burlap, and claws strolled past them. Ludicra lumbered quickly down the swaying bridge, trying to ignore the gossip from her so-called friends. "Can you believe it?" they went on. "She thought she was going to marry our hero, Rollo. Ha! What a billy goat!"

The others snickered loudly enough for Ludicra to hear them. There was a time not long ago when these foul-weather fur bags had basked in her shadow, eager to please her. Now Ludicra was a laughingstock, just because that stupid Rollo had deserted her. Of course, he had deserted *all* of them—trolls, ogres, and gnomes alike—by refusing to become their king. Instead he had run off to the Bonny Woods to return the dead body of his little fairy friend, Clipper.

But the stout troll had trouble believing most of what she had heard about Rollo lately. Of course, he had been trollnapped along with half the village in order to build a bridge across the Great Chasm. That had never happened, but Rollo had caught the eye of the village's departed sorcerer, Stygius Rex, being one of the few who could fly. After that, the stories about him had become hard to believe, sounding more like legend than fact.

Had Rollo really flown across the Great Chasm—to battle elves and befriend a fairy named Clipper? How could he desert Stygius Rex and become an outlaw, only to turn around and lead an army of trolls in revolt against the sorcerer? They had defeated Stygius Rex and his dreadful ghouls—that much was apparently true, because they were gone. Everyone, even the ogres, revered Rollo's name and wanted to make him king of all Bonespittle.

All Ludicra could remember was the sweet troll who had followed her around, looking dopey with love. Where had *he* gone? More than anything, she wanted to be queen of all Bonespittle, but she kind of missed that goofy Rollo. He didn't have enough hair, humps, warts, or knots, but he was as big and strong as an ogre. He was funny, too.

But if he were here now, I would take him apart, snout hair by snout hair! the young troll decided.

Ludicra stomped her foot angrily, and that was a mistake, because the bridge plank broke under her weight. The plump troll crashed right through a second and third plank, but she managed to catch the bottom rope with her hairy armpit. Her feet dangled dangerously over the brackish water as she grasped at wispy fog with her free hand. On the other bridge, her friends shrieked with alarm and rushed to her aid. That was the second mistake.

Their weight caused more of the planks to crack, and the whole suspension bridge began to slump toward the black swamp. Shrieking, her rescuers scrambled back to the nearest spit of mud and tree stumps, where they huddled in helpless fear.

Ludicra couldn't understand their panic, until she saw the slimy water part beneath her. A huge tentacle curled upward, gingerly tickling her feet. Since it was night, she couldn't see anything but that one sucker-lined appendage, but it was enough to send her into kicking mode. With no place to put her feet, and nothing to grab but slippery rope, she could only flail helplessly in the air. Suddenly the giant tentacle rose up, wrapped around her ankle, and jerked her down into the gloom.

The rope under her arm broke, and Ludicra plummeted into the vile liquid. She thrashed about as six more tentacles wrapped themselves around various body parts, including her mouth. That was a mistake for the sucker fish, because Ludicra was already stinking mad. She sunk her big fangs into the slimy appendage, and the monster recoiled in pain.

Someone above her helped by lowering a lantern, and she spotted a root on the muddy bank. With a determined lunge, the troll grabbed the root and began to drag herself out of the foul bog.

The sucker continued to squeeze her torso and try to drag her under, but Ludicra wasn't going to fight the fish in the water; she'd take care of it on land. Her friends yelled encouragement from above, and one or two reached down to help her. Ludicra ignored them, because she was mad at them . . . mad at life—and especially mad at Rollo. Snorting and grunting, the muddy troll dragged herself from the muck of the Dismal Swamp, under the broken bridge in Troll Town.

The sucker fish had the good sense to slither back into the swamp before she could grab it, so that it didn't become her breakfast. Ludicra lay panting at the side of someone's hovel, until finally she found the strength to stand.

Staggering to her feet, she roared, "Isn't someone supposed to repair these lousy bridges?"

The old troll holding the lantern leaned over and nodded. Then he lifted the light close enough to his face for Ludicra to see that it was Krunkle, the master bridge builder. He looked sickened and ashamed.

"Nobody repairs the bridges anymore," muttered Krunkle. "Everyone stopped work when Stygius Rex troll-napped half the village. They never went back to work, and neither did the ones who hid. Now nobody works! The ogres are not here to force us, and there's still food left over from the sorcerer's camp. But when all the leech pie runs out . . ."

The old troll just shook his head, his batwing ears flopping back and forth.

"Help me up!" snapped Ludicra, pointing to her former friends. Enough of them bent down to lift her to the top of the knoll, where a sizable crowd had gathered.

Ludicra brushed the mire from her burlap dress and matted fur, and found a leech squirming to get away. She plucked and ate the critter, then looked around at her fellow trolls. They stared at her, slack-jawed and so bored that someone falling into the bog was a night's rich entertainment.

What Krunkle said was *true*! she realized. Since Rollo left, they had lost their direction. They still woke up every night and went out, but they wandered around Troll Town like a bunch of ghouls, with no ambition and no desire. For the first time since anyone could remember, the trolls had no boss, no overlords. But this freedom had brought them laziness, not happiness.

She looked around for Krunkle and saw that the builder was roping off the section of collapsed bridge. In chalk, he drew the sign for UNDER REPAIR on a stump, but Ludicra doubted that it would get repaired anytime soon. Luckily, the village was nothing but a spiderweb of tattered bridges, and most of them would still hold up a troll's weight. *But for how long?*

"We need to get Rollo back," declared Ludicra. *So I can be queen,* she thought.

"I know we need Rollo," said Krunkle with a shrug of

his bent, hairy shoulders. "But how? He went back across the Great Chasm—and he can fly, but we can't."

"Maybe there's a way across we don't know about," said Ludicra with determination. "We can't give up so easily. He's been gone over a fortnight, and he should have been back by now. Maybe he's in trouble. Even if we can't find him, it'll be better than sitting around here, trimming our talons. It will be one of those whadya-call-its. A—"

"Quest!" called another voice. Ludicra turned to see Crawfleece, Rollo's big sister, muscling her way through the crowd. *Surely, here is one troll who is brave enough to go with me!*

"You'll join me on this quest?" asked Ludicra hopefully.

"Yes, but we'll need everyone's support," said Crawfleece. "There's a chance we might start a war with the fairies and elves if we cross the chasm. The ogres are still better warriors than we are, and we'll need a few of them. Plus we should ask them for some horses. Who's that gnome—the one in charge?"

"Runt," answered Krunkle with a sigh. "But I don't think he's any more in charge than I am."

"Fine, we'll get help," said Ludicra with a snort. "But I'm going to be in charge."

Crawfleece narrowed her piggy eyes at Ludicra and said, "We're doing this for everyone, not just you. Mainly, we're doing it for Rollo. We just want him to be happy, right? And I'm older than you, so *I* should be the leader."

"Get yourself your own party to lead!" snapped Ludicra. "Anybody who comes with me has to know that I'm in charge. And the horses will be to carry supplies, not for eating."

Crawfleece scowled, and Ludicra smiled at her. "I'm going to marry your brother and be queen of Bonespittle someday, and I don't want my subjects to think I ate the pack animals."

"Whatever you say," muttered Crawfleece.

The would-be queen continued to smile, thinking about the feast they would have after she rescued Rollo. That would be the same night when the grateful king will ask her to be his bride.

Fungus Meadows certainly lived up to its name, with lovely patches of gray-streaked fungus stretching across a plain of thistle bushes. It was the most beautiful place in all of Bonespittle, or so they said. Ludicra decided that it looked like a mountain hollow after a sooty snowstorm, the kind that swept northward from the volcano. They said one could eat the fungus, but it appeared that the fungus was eating everything else.

Seeing as how it was such a desirable place, Ludicra and Crawfleece expected to see someone living in Fungus Meadows. They'd always heard that the cream of ogre society lived in the vale, and Rollo's father claimed that trolls had once lived here. Now it appeared as if the place was deserted, except for a few skeletal remains of old tents, their tattered hides flapping in the wind. The two female trolls' feet squished heavily on the fungus, which gave off a putrid smell redolent of dank dungeons.

They passed by several deep burrows as they crossed the vale. It was tempting to peer inside these dark holes and wonder what creatures lurked beneath the soil. Perhaps ogres and gnomes alike were underground at this time of day. But it was almost night. *Shouldn't there be some kind of sentry or watch?* Ludicra wondered.

"This can't be Fungus Meadows," said Crawfleece with a sneer.

"It's right where the road led us," answered Ludicra. "This is it. What else would this place be called?"

"Then why are these tents all torn up?" demanded Crawfleece.

Ludicra shrugged. "Why are our bridges falling apart? We live in weird times. Modern Bonespittle is not the land of our parents. You've got a brother who can fly and defeat a powerful sorcerer, and fairies turn out to be so cute they make you gag. I'm afraid that elves are going to be cuddly too."

"Do you really think the gnomes will help us on this mad quest?" asked Crawfleece.

Ludicra motioned around the desolate landscape. "What have they got to lose?"

After a few more minutes of walking, Ludicra stopped at the biggest burrow she had seen yet. It was a wide tunnel that sloped downward into the fungus and dark loam beneath. "I think we'll go down here," she said.

"Down there?" asked Crawfleece with a gulp. "We'll get stuck."

"Just imagine it's one of our hovels," said Ludicra, dropping to her knees. "We may have to go a little deeper to find anyone, but we'll find them."

Ludicra crawled headfirst into the burrow, which was lined with dripping vines and a few odd bones. It seemed initially that the tunnel slumped downward at a sensible angle, but it soon turned into a muddy chute. With a squeal, the plump troll flopped onto her stomach and slid down the burrow until she shot into a dark space. Ludicra rolled into a big ball just before she crashed into a pile of damp straw. She lay panting on the cold muddy floor, trying to catch her breath, when she heard another shriek above her.

The troll scrambled out of the way an instant before Crawfleece came barreling in from the hole above. With a grunt, she plowed into the straw and came up sputtering.

"Shh!" cautioned Ludicra.

Crawfleece stopped chattering, and both trolls glanced at a tiny pool of light at the end of the passageway to their left. The underground lair was a labyrinth, with passages curling up and down, left and right. Getting that torch seemed like a good idea, and they shuffled toward it. Ludicra started out in a crouch, but she soon found that she could stand upright. Only her long hairy ears scraped the top of the cavern.

As they neared the flickering torch, Ludicra and Crawfleece saw ogre markings on the wall, plus more tunnels curling into the darkness. "It's kind of dry here," whispered Crawfleece. "You know, this isn't a bad place. If the gnomes and ogres have cleared out, I say we claim it for the trolls."

"First we find Rollo," insisted Ludicra. "Do you want to take the torch?"

"It doesn't do us much good hanging on the wall." With that, Crawfleece grabbed the burning torch and lifted it from its iron holder. At once, the holder snapped back into the wall, and the torch went out.

"Uh-oh," said Ludicra, a moment before she heard whooshing sounds.

From the shadows on every side of them, nets came rushing toward them, spreading open. The trolls threw up their hands and tried to duck, but it was too late. A number of nets ensnared them, and their own struggling dragged them to the ground. Somewhere a bell began to peal a warning, but no horde of ogres descended upon them.

"What? How?" shouted Ludicra.

"Ogre crossbows," panted Crawfleece. "They must have been hidden in the walls, and we set off the trap."

"We?" asked Ludicra.

"Okay, I did it. But at least now they know we're here."

Ludicra scowled. "Unless, like you said, this place is deserted. Hey, I've got a knife somewhere." She twisted in the thick nets, getting more entangled with every move-ment. "If I can just get to my pouch—"

"Save your energy," whispered Crawfleece. "Someone's coming."

Twisted like a piece of gopher jerky, Ludicra managed to look under her arm. A hulking figure loomed in the shadows of a lower tunnel, and she heard his sloshing footsteps coming closer. He meandered toward them, bouncing a big club on his massive shoulder. The hulk lifted the baffles on his lantern, letting light spill upon them.

"What have we here?" he growled. "Visitors? What tribe are ye from?" His massive curved tusks glimmered in the light as the ogre bent down to study them. His red eyes widened in wonder. "Trolls?"

"You were expecting elves?" asked Ludicra. "We're here to see the ones in charge."

"In charge!" The ogre snorted in derisive laughter. "Don't you recognize me? I'm Chomp, formerly captain of the guard . . . when there was something left to guard." He pulled a knife and snarled at them, but Ludicra could see that he looked older and thinner. Plus he moved stiffly, as if he'd been battered in a fight.

"I should skin the two of you," grumbled Chomp, "for all the trouble you trolls have caused us."

"Trouble?" asked Ludicra. "Weren't the ogres ready to make Rollo their king? Weren't you glad he freed us from Stygius Rex?"

Chomp grunted. "We were for a while. But then Rollo was gone, and not too many ogres ever met him. All they knew was that one night, they woke up and the sorcerer and his ghouls were gone. They were free to do whatever they wanted. Do you think they wanted to watch over trolls all day long? Or build more barracks? No, they wanted to *fight* each other. The old tribal loyalties sprang up, and now we've got a dozen different warlords trying to hold on to little fiefdoms. Thanks a lot, you dumb trolls."

"We're going to go find Rollo," vowed Ludicra. "And when we bring him back, things will be set right."

The grizzled ogre narrowed his red eyes thoughtfully and peered at the young troll. "By *you,* little one?"

"By all of us," she answered bravely. "Captain Chomp, you must come along with us to find Rollo. You know that he's the only one who can unite us. We're going to talk to Runt, so we can get the supplies and help we need."

"You can talk to Runt all you want," muttered Chomp, "but there are no supplies, unless you've got an army big enough to steal them."

"No horses?" asked Crawfleece sadly.

He shook his head. "Ate them last week."

Ludicra gulped and went on, "What do you say, Captain Chomp? Are you with us?"

"Rollo might be dead, you know," said the ogre softly. "Might be the folks of the Bonny Woods don't like to see dead fairies."

"But he had that knife," said Crawfleece. "The black one, which Stygius Rex used to make ghouls. He was going to bring Clipper back to life!"

The big ogre shivered for a moment. "Ah, the serpent knife. Somehow that doesn't bring me much comfort. This journey . . . it won't be an easy one."

"Then cut us out of this net, so we can get started," snapped Ludicra.

Chomp just shook his shaggy head and laughed. "I guess you're Rollo's mate all right. And he deserves you."

CHAPTER 2

ALLIES AND ENEMIES

RUNT SCRATCHED THE SCRAGGLY HAIRS ON HIS BULBOUS head, which was large for someone only three feet tall. The elder gnome scuttled across his untidy lair, his talons scraping on the dried mud. Ludicra sat down and scrunched lower, because her ears kept scraping against the mold on the ceiling. *Mold is meant to be eaten, not worn,* she thought. Crawfleece and Chomp were having an even harder time fitting into the gnome's hovel.

Rollo's ogre friend, Chomp, had brought them to the scribe, and Ludicra had told him about her plan to rescue Rollo and drag him home. Now she waited for the gnome's reaction, but all he did was pace his tiny lair. Chomp grunted impatiently, and Crawfleece combed the floor looking for grubs.

Runt finally stopped pacing and nodded sagely. "Yes, yes, we have to do something to bring Rollo back. We can't let things go on as they have. There's no one in Bonespittle who the subjects fear . . . or respect. What do you think, Captain Chomp?"

The big ogre was sitting cross-legged on the floor of the cramped quarters. "I think it's a stupid idea, and nobody who goes over there will ever come back. On the other claw, it was the trolls who got rid of Stygius Rex, and I say it's *their* duty to restore order to Bonespittle! So I'll help find Rollo and drag him home, even though I doubt if any of us will live through this venture."

The little gnome scrunched his rubbery face. "Argh, these are strange times we live in! The fate of the land depends upon a troll who has run away. And the last time he ran away, he overthrew Stygius Rex. I should go with you to look for him, but I'm too old. And someone has to remain in charge."

Chomp snorted, as if doubting that anyone was in charge.

Runt ignored him and scuttled toward Ludicra and Crawfleece. "According to our legends," he whispered, "there *is* a secret passageway from the lip of the Great Chasm to the bottom. No living gnome could tell you where it is, though a team of our miners might be able to find it. But I have no idea what you'll find at the bottom, or how you could climb the other side to the Bonny Woods. Even if you don't all die horribly, as Chomp thinks you will, this quest could take years to finish."

"It's better than sitting around and doing nothing!" declared Ludicra. "The sooner we get started, the sooner we find Rollo." She tried to stand but banged her head on the low ceiling in Runt's hovel. "Ow!"

The elder gnome held up his hand. "Don't rush off, child. Let me assemble a team of gnomes to go with you. One of them will be my nephew, Gnat. He's very strange—he *likes* to be above ground. And he's been thirsting for adventure."

"Plus we need supplies and more fighting ogres," Chomp cut in. "I wonder what my old friend Weevil is doing. Last I heard, she was with Sergeant Skull."

"Skull is a bucket of unspoiled cream!" shouted Runt, his big nose twitching angrily. He glanced at his guests. "Excuse my language, but he's one of the warlords who is fighting to take over Bonespittle. I doubt if he'll help us bring back Rollo."

"We'll leave Sergeant Skull alone," agreed Chomp.

In the bright glare of daylight, when no self-respecting citizen of Bonespittle should have been walking about, thirteen gnomes crawled out of their burrows. Two trolls and an ogre joined them, and they all stood squinting in the harsh sunlight of Fungus Meadows. Sunshine glinted off the white blight covering the ground as if it were freshly fallen snow.

Warily, Ludicra surveyed the gnomes in their lumpy

helmet lanterns and tool belts, loaded with hammers, picks, and ropes. The ogres were burdened with weapons and shields, and the trolls carried general supplies. She hefted her own backpack, thinking that they had a long walk ahead of them. *As a future queen,* thought Ludicra, *I should have someone carry my backpack for me.*

A brash, hairy gnome marched up to Ludicra and offered his taloned hand. "Hello, I'm Gnat! My uncle is Runt, the scribe."

"Yes, Runt told us about you," she answered, squinting down at him. "They say that you like to be above ground."

"I like to visit, but I wouldn't want to live here," answered the young gnome, looking around at the bright landscape of fungi and weeds. "But I know the land and the old legends—I'll help you find that tunnel. One more thing—if you want to talk to the miners, you'd better talk to me first."

The gnome lowered his voice and made them lean down to hear him say, "They think *I'm* in charge of this expedition."

"Do they now?" asked Ludicra with a sniff. "You wee folk are here for only one reason—to find me a way down and across the Great Chasm. If you fail, we'll leave you behind—I don't care *who* your uncle is."

The young gnome lowered his hairy brow, snorted, and gnashed his fangs. Captain Chomp laughed and said, "Gnat, you had best learn that true love guides this quest. Ludicra may not be the brains of this party, but she is the heart."

"And don't you forget it," said Ludicra.

Gnat bowed to the big ogre. "As you say, Captain."

"Don't call me 'captain,'" grumbled Chomp. "Until we get to the Great Chasm, I'm just a guard with no name. We don't want Skull or any of the warlords to know what we're doing, so we have a story. This is a work crew, and you and the trolls are going to repair an old privy—put a bridge over it or something. We'll meet Weevil at the ford across the Rawchill River."

"Horses?" asked Crawfleece eagerly.

"If she can steal any from Sergeant Skull, maybe," answered the ogre. "But I wouldn't count on it." Chomp squinted into the sun and began pounding through the sand on his beefy legs. "This way! Watch your step, it's awfully light out here!"

The hardy band followed a winding path for half a day, seeing nothing but ruined tents and hovels, some of them still smoldering. Broken battle-axes, maces, and spears stuck out of the dark sand, and some large burrows had been reduced to craters. Crawfleece strode beside Ludicra, her lantern jaw hanging agape at the sight of another wrecked village.

"Everything we heard is true," whispered Crawfleece. "The ogres are fighting each other, getting vengeance for old scores. If they unite and decide to come after us—" She didn't need to finish her thought.

"We've all suffered," said Ludicra. "That's why the

ogres will want to make peace and follow Rollo . . . once we get him back."

"How can you be so sure?" asked Crawfleece.

Ludicra snorted with derision. "Well, they'll just have to. He'll be king, won't he?"

"But nobody remembers having a king."

"It will be just like having a sorcerer," answered Ludicra, "only everybody in the kingdom will *like* him instead of hate him."

"When you put it that way, it almost sounds unnatural," said Crawfleece with a shiver. "I guess I'm having a hard time accepting this, when it's my little brother we're talking about."

"His actions are heroic," insisted Ludicra. "The potential for greatness is there."

"What if he doesn't marry you?" asked Crawfleece with a sly smile.

Ludicra snorted. "Then he'll be like sludge pudding with no worms. He'll be worthless! Rollo needs to listen to me."

"I don't think my brother is listening to anyone but himself," muttered Crawfleece.

Ludicra stopped suddenly and cupped her hand to her pointed ear. "Do you hear that?"

"Yes, it's the sound of the river. We're still maybe two hours away."

"Three hours away," said Chomp, striding past them. "Let's get there before dark. Move it!"

The little gnomes scuttled past, huffing and puffing under the weight of their tool belts. Still, everyone kept a good pace until they could see the fog and the cold slash of purple water just ahead of them. The sun was beginning to dip behind the hills, making their shadows as long as the gnarled roots growing in the crusty soil. There were twisted trees and scraggly bushes along the banks of the Rawchill River, but it all seemed frozen and bleak . . . except for the dark shapes moving in the mist.

"Remember," whispered Chomp, "I'm a guard, and you're my work crew." The ogre strode ahead of them, letting the trolls and gnomes sheepishly follow. The figures in the fog raised their weapons, but they lowered them after a few words with Chomp. With his club, he waved the rest of the party forward.

Ludicra counted four big ogres and one solitary shape who knelt at the edge of the river, watching the choppy rapids. A lanky female ogre strolled up to them and studied the travelers with amusement.

"I'm Weevil," she said, "another friend of Rollo's. I must be crazy for listening to Chomp and giving up my command, but I miss that dumb troll. Listen, we must cross this river quickly, because Skull will find out we're gone. We, er . . . borrowed some supplies from him. He may already be after us, so we have to cross before dark—"

"With no horses, how can we get across?" asked Crawfleece.

Weevil clicked her tusks and looked back at the coursing river. "We'll run a rope across the ford and pull ourselves hand over hand. It will be unpleasant, but ogres and trolls are tall enough to make it. I'm just worried about the gnomes."

"I thought you said you had a flying troll with you," said Chomp.

Weevil shrugged. "Well, he's one of those who flew with Rollo. I haven't seen him fly lately, but he insisted on coming with us." She pointed toward the solitary figure standing by the water's edge.

"Who is it?" demanded Ludicra, stepping forward.

A smallish troll walked from the mist and grinned at them with crooked fangs. "Never fear, Filbum is here!"

"You can't fly!" scoffed Crawfleece. "You can barely do a night's work."

"I've been practicing!" he countered. "And hasn't anyone told you that I flew across this very river?"

"*With* Rollo," answered Ludicra.

"And Rollo learned to fly alone, didn't he?" replied Filbum, undaunted. "We practiced flying over this river so that we could fly over the Great Chasm one day. And Rollo succeeded! I tell you, I've been practicing. Now tie a length of rope around my waist, and I'll put the other end on the far bank."

Filbum pointed into a fog so ominous that no one could see the other side of the Rawchill River. What they could see of the river had chunks of ice floating in it.

From the gathering of gnomes, Gnat stepped forward and uncoiled a rope. "I keep hearing about trolls who can fly, and now I want to see one!" Gnat looped the rope around Filbum's middle, formed a knot, and tightened it so hard that the troll let out a belch.

Filbum looked down at the rope, then at the expectant faces, and gulped. "Right," he said, rubbing his stomach. "Get a good hold on the rope. . . . I don't want to go so fast that I yank it from your hands."

"I doubt that will happen," said Chomp, grabbing the free end from Gnat. "Go on, while we still have daylight."

The troll nodded and walked purposefully into the fog, which clung to the Rawchill River like slime stew. When he reached the bank, Filbum lowered his head and began to mutter to himself, while he pounded his chest like a drum. It was a very impressive ritual, and the others edged closer. None of them wanted to miss seeing a troll fly . . . or land in the frigid river.

Finally Filbum lifted his arms as if they were wings, and he soared into the fog. Losing sight of the troll, Ludicra and the others rushed forward just in time to hear a scream and a very loud splash. The swift current nearly ripped the rope from Chomp's hands, but he hung on until Weevil and Crawfleece could grab it. Pulling with all their might, the trio managed to drag a wet, shivering troll out of the frosty mire.

"Th-th-th—that's *cold!*" shrieked Filbum as he curled into a chattering ball.

"What happened to the flying part?" asked Gnat. The curious gnome knelt down to retrieve his rope.

"D-d-d-didn't you see me fly?" croaked Filbum. "A f-f-few feet?"

They all shook their heads and looked doubtfully at one another. So Ludicra asked, "While you were in the water, could you touch the bottom?"

"Yes, but I was off-balance," Filbum answered, shivering. "It's maybe waist-deep."

As they considered what to do next, silence fell around the band huddled on the edge of the Rawchill River. Ludicra heard the clank of armor somewhere in the mist, and she whirled around at the same moment Chomp did.

The captain drew his club and met the attack of a screaming ogre who leaped from the fog. Weevil and the other four ogres drew their weapons and met an equal number in battle. Luckily, the attackers were confused and hesitant in the fog, unsure of who was friend, who foe. When Chomp threw one of them into the icy rapids, two of them slunk away.

"Quick!" shouted Ludicra. "Everyone, grab a gnome!"

Ludicra snatched Gnat off his feet before he could even protest, then she waded into the icy depths. Crawfleece was right behind her, carrying two squirming gnomes. Even Filbum splashed back into the rapids with a gnome under his arm. As the grunts and clangs of battle echoed from the mist, the three trolls struggled through the fierce current.

"Don't drop me!" squeaked Gnat, his voice almost lost above the roar of the water.

"Better hang on then," she rasped.

The gnome instantly perched on her shoulders and grabbed her head, covering her eyes and mouth. Ludicra bit him, and he jerked one hand back. But that didn't do much good—she still couldn't see more than a few feet in either direction with the fog covering both banks. So Ludicra used her long ears, knowing the noise of battle was behind her.

Soon she lost all feeling from her toes up to her chest, and only fear made her legs keep churning.

Ludicra was so numb from plodding through the surging, waist-deep rapids that she didn't even know she had reached the bank until Gnat leaped off her shoulders. The gnome scrambled onto the muddy ground and kissed it, while Ludicra collapsed in the reeds. She had just enough strength left to drag her frozen legs out of the water.

She heard a grunt and turned to see Crawfleece dump a couple of gnomes onto dry land. Then Rollo's big sister waded back into the freezing whitecaps to pull Filbum and his passenger to safety. For a while, the three trolls and four gnomes lay shivering on the misty bank, curled into pathetic balls. No sounds of fighting echoed from the far bank, noted Ludicra, so maybe the battle was over. Would any of the ogres make it across the Rawchill River?

Her question was answered a few moments later when Chomp, Weevil, and two more ogres staggered to the bank, each carrying two gnomes. The big ogres collapsed on land, breathing hard and shivering, and no one spoke until everyone had caught their breath.

"We left two ogres behind?" asked Ludicra.

Chomp nodded grimly. "And there were three gnomes we couldn't carry."

"What about Skull's warriors?" asked Ludicra, peering into the ominous fog that blanketed the frigid river. "Will they come after us?"

"I doubt it," answered Weevil with a loud cough. "They're not as stupid as we are. But they saw us. . . . We'll be marked ogres in Bonespittle from now on."

"Don't worry, you'll be the *only* ogres where we're going," answered Filbum.

Ludicra looked away from the river toward the wild plain that led to the Great Chasm. Shadows were deepening across the barren landscape, making it look even craggier and more foreboding than usual. "It's getting dark," said Ludicra. "Why don't we get away from the river, build a fire, and dry out before we leave. Otherwise we'll freeze on the trail."

"That m-m-makes sense to me," said Gnat, shivering. He pointed to his fellow gnomes. "All of you, g-g-gather firewood and kindling, and dry your flints." The gnomes rose on their stubby legs and shook themselves like dogs, then they scattered in different directions.

Weevil sat up and brushed the dampness off her fur. "We

could sleep at night and travel by day, to avoid being seen."

"No!" said Ludicra. "There won't be any sleeping until we find Rollo."

The ogres and trolls looked warily at one another and scrunched their toothy faces. They had just started their quest, and already Ludicra could see the doubt and fear in their eyes. How could she keep them together? The only fear she felt was for Rollo, and the only doubt she had was that they would reach him in time.

Wherever he was.

CHAPTER 3

NARROW ESCAPES

ROLLO SQUIRMED IN THE GIANT SPIDERWEB, WHERE HE HAD been stuck for almost a week. Luckily, he had yet to see the giant spider who had built this atrocious trap, but it had to be a big one. The sticky strands stretched in every direction for as far as he could see.

In one tightly bound hand, he gently clasped the small coffinwood box that held Clipper's body. His other hand was empty but just as surely stuck in the rubbery strands. For days he had tried to reach the black serpent knife on his belt, but the web was like a living thing that seemed to grow tighter wherever he pulled it. Getting ahold of that knife seemed like his only hope, and he had to do it before he got too weak.

The young troll thought back upon the stupidity that had

landed him here. Upon reaching the Bonny Woods, Rollo
had promptly been attacked by elves with arrows, so he had
flown to high ground. There were craggy outcroppings of
rock scattered around the woods, and he had zoomed into a
narrow canyon without looking. A second later, he had been
firmly stuck in this monstrous web, surrounded by the flaky
remains of other hapless birds and fairies. Rollo understood
why no fairies came buzzing around to investigate him, and
the rocks were too steep for elves to climb.

They probably preferred to feed him to the spider, anyway.

Somewhere in the rocks above him, there was a spring,
and cool water dribbled down the web strands into this
mouth. So he wasn't going to die of thirst. But Rollo was
getting powerfully hungry—and very weak. He wasn't sure
how well he could fly, and it was a long drop down to the
Bonny Woods. Still, he had to get that knife and try to cut
himself out. Since nobody was going to rescue him, it was
his only chance.

Rollo heard some gravel skitter down the rock wall,
and he tried to turn his head in that direction. Except for
wind and dripping water, it was the first sound the troll had
heard in days. Then he felt a vibration coursing through the
web structure, and it tickled his entire body. But he wasn't
laughing, especially when he felt the weird vibration again
and again.

Now the sticky strands of web were almost bouncing,
and Rollo twisted his whole body around to see the source.

A dark shape dropped down and hung in the narrow canyon, blocking out the feeble rays of the setting sun. Rollo peered at the fuzzy ball of a creature, wondering what it was. When it stretched eight long, hairy legs, he knew that the owner of the web had returned. The giant spider was as big as Old Belch, the sorcerer Stygius Rex's riding toad!

That was when the troll began to shout and scream, hoping to scare the beast away. But the more he struggled and howled, the more curious the spider became; it edged forward, tickling the strands around his waist.

In desperation, Rollo used his teeth to gnaw on the strand nearest him, which was also attached to his arm. At the same time, he told himself this was like fighting a sucker fish or a snapper in the bottom of the swamp. If he didn't fight for all he was worth, he was no more than spider dinner.

After he gnawed through the foul strand, Rollo felt some give in the web, and he looked back to see the spider. It opened a horrible gaping mouth and snapped at him with long mandibles that looked like knives. Shiny liquid, maybe venom, gleamed on the spider's sharp fangs.

Roaring and howling, Rollo struggled in the cords with all his might. He finally pulled his arm free, and reached for the black knife in his belt. The troll hated that knife, but it did come in handy sometimes.

The mammoth spider stalked him, bouncing the web, and Rollo screamed like a banshee. He slashed at his bindings, and the black knife seemed to melt them like butter. Rollo even managed to free the precious box in which Clipper's body rested, but he had to be careful not to drop it. As the spider loomed over him—looking like a hill with tree trunks as legs—he slashed at the web around his own legs.

When the spider leaped, Rollo was able to free one leg and kick the monster. He had no idea where his heel landed, but green ooze splattered his face. The troll licked some of it off—he was really hungry, then went back to kicking the spider with all his strength. Under their weight and with many strands broken, the web began to sag. Rollo felt as if he were in an old hammock that was about to snap, and he tried to remember how to fly.

The beast used one of its hairy legs to slash at him, and that was enough to break the web for good. With a shout, Rollo plummeted down, and the great spider swung for a moment but caught the web with one of its other legs. Rollo didn't have such luck as he went crashing down the cliff face and through the scraggly bushes. He gripped Clipper's box to his chest and tried to muster the concentration needed to fly. The best he could do was slow his fall just before he struck the top of the trees.

The troll still went crashing through the branches. Between painful blows, he tried to protect the coffin and the black serpent knife. With a thud, Rollo landed on the forest floor, and that was the last thing he remembered.

* * *

Something sharp prodded Rollo in the shoulder, joining aches and pains all over his body. There was something different about this pain, though, and it was enough to drag the young troll back to consciousness. He looked up to see several bearded, flint-eyed elves looking down at him; each one had an arrow cocked in his bow. Rollo tried to sit up—to escape—but his limbs refused to move. That was when the injured troll realized there were ropes all over him—he was tied up neater than a roasted slug.

When the elves saw he wasn't going to escape from their bindings, they lowered their bows. He realized that they had his box and the black knife, and were studying the two objects warily.

"Don't open the box," he warned, "unless you know what you're doing."

The golden-haired elf who had the coffin suddenly dropped it to the ground. "Is it a trap?" he asked. "What dirty plot is this from you foul folk?"

Rollo wheezed painfully and twisted around to see all his captors. "It holds a body . . . that of a fairy named Clipper. Her body has been perfectly preserved, because the box is made of coffinwood."

The elves looked at one another with disgust. They were a mix of males and females, all of them slight of build, no more than five feet tall, wearing green garb that blended into the forest. Several of them kept guard in the nearby trees.

"You kill a fairy, then preserve her body?" asked a

female elf. "What kind of fiends are you?"

"Do you plan to eat her later?" asked another.

"No, no!" Rollo quickly assured them. "You also have the black serpent knife. That belonged to Stygius Rex—he used it to raise the dead and create ghouls."

At once, the elf holding the black knife tossed it into the dirt. "Everything they own is cursed!" he shouted.

"You don't understand!" wailed Rollo. "Clipper was my friend! She helped me defeat Stygius Rex and free the citizens of Bonespittle from his tyranny. I brought Clipper back to the Bonny Woods, because I promised her I would. But if there's a chance to restore her to life, don't you think we should seize it?"

The grim-faced elves looked at one another and then at the objects lying in the leaves. *Which is greater,* wondered Rollo, *their fear or their curiosity?*

A red-bearded elf muscled his way through the throng. "Don't believe a word he says!" snapped the elf. "There's no magic in this ugly creature, or in his stolen goods. He's just trying to delay us from punishing him. Hand me that box!"

"Yes, Prince Thatch." The blond-haired elf quickly retrieved the wooden container and handed it to his master.

Thatch studied the box from every angle, then prodded the latch with the tip of his arrow. "It's probably booby-trapped," he muttered.

"It's not trapped," scoffed Rollo. "Hand it to me, and I'll open it."

"Yes, you'd like that," said Thatch with a sneer. "Filch, keep your eye on him."

"Yes, Prince Thatch." The blond-haired elf pointed an arrow at the fallen troll and smiled. "We'll stop his evil trickery."

With his arrowhead, Thatch cautiously pried open the latch, then lifted the lid. The red-haired elf gasped when he saw what was inside, and his hands began to shake. Some elves pressed forward to see, while others retreated in fear. All who were brave enough to peer into the box let out gasps of wonder, and a few grinned.

Lying on the ground, Rollo couldn't see his friend Clipper, but he had sneaked a glance into the box before. The fairy looked perfectly alive—more beautiful than ever—only sleeping peacefully. There was no sign that Clipper had drowned at the hands of Stygius Rex.

"My lord," breathed Filch, "she does look well preserved. Perhaps he was telling the truth."

"Find me a mage," pleaded Rollo. "Someone who can wield the black knife and bring Clipper back to life!"

"Silence!" The prince glared at Rollo, then he slammed the lid shut on the box. "We won't use the troll for target practice . . . just yet. Let's take him to see our beloved Melinda, the Enchantress Mother."

There were nods and mutterings of agreement, and Rollo let out his breath. Was he finally going to see someone who could help him?

"Roll him up and put him on a pole," ordered Prince Thatch. "Scouts, you go ahead. Make sure to look out for birds!"

"Look out for birds?" asked Rollo puzzledly. "What's the matter with the birds?"

Thatch sneered at him. "As if you didn't know! Ever since you and your vile master came here, there has been war between the birds and the fairies. Even we elves can't travel alone, because flocks of birds will attack us. You know this is your horrible handiwork."

Rollo started to protest, but then he remembered that Stygius Rex had stayed in the Bonny Woods after he fled. Plus the birds had been discontented with their lot. Given such an opportunity, the sorcerer was more than capable of starting a war between the flying creatures of the Bonny Woods.

"Incoming!" shouted one of the elven guards.

The elves scattered for cover under the trees as a noisy flock of birds swooped through the forest, letting loose with white gobs that splattered everywhere, drenching the hidden elves. Rollo closed his eyes and tried to burrow into the ground, but he couldn't escape the onslaught either.

When the attack was over, the soiled elves glared at the departing flock of birds. "I hate this war," muttered Filch.

"Please believe me," said Rollo, "I have nothing to do with this." The bedraggled troll cleared his throat and looked appealingly at his captors. "I'm really hungry. I don't suppose you have any food on you?"

"Pick him up!" ordered Prince Thatch. "It's getting dark."

Roughly, the elves shoved a pole between Rollo's bound limbs. It took eight of them to lift and carry the big troll, and they stumbled often. He was banged against the branches, piling bruises upon bruises, but it was still better than walking, Rollo figured. As they marched, many elven warriors kept their bows ready, guarding against birds, or perhaps more trolls falling from the sky. Prince Thatch kept the coffinwood box and black serpent knife clutched tightly to his chest.

CHAPTER 4

NOT-SO-GREAT CHASM

B Y NIGHTFALL, A WEARY BAND OF GRIMY TROLLS, BRUTISH ogres, and diminutive gnomes staggered to the rim of the Great Chasm. Many of them crawled on their hands and knees, afraid to fall off or just too tired to stand. Even by twilight, they could see the immense, gaping darkness of the chasm. The Bonespittle side was nothing but craggy wasteland, and the far side was an endless canopy of treetops.

For the first time, Ludicra felt a pang of helplessness. Surely, getting to the bottom of this monstrous gorge would be nearly impossible, if it even had a bottom. And climbing up the other side to the Bonny Woods might be an even more ridiculous thought. From this vantage point, the chasm appeared to be unimaginably deep and huge—an obstacle none of them could ever conquer.

Gnat the gnome cleared his throat and looked doubtfully at her. "Are you sure that Rollo flew across *there?*"

"He brought back a fairy, didn't he?" asked Ludicra.

"It's really no wider than the Rawchill River," said Filbum, his voice squeaking a little. "And we flew across that."

"Yeah, you can fly," said Chomp, slapping the young troll on the back. "Give it a try."

Chomp's slap on the back nearly pushed Filbum off the edge, and the troll skidded to a stop. "Thanks, Captain Chomp, but I have to practice some more." Filbum quickly backed away from the gaping gorge.

Ludicra put her claws on her plump hips and glared at the rest of her party. "It won't do us any good to stand here and stare at it. You gnomes, get to work on finding the passageway down. Where will you begin?"

Gnat gathered the other nine gnomes together in a line, then he conferred with a gray-haired elder named Flint. After getting his answer, Gnat turned to the trolls and ogres and said, "The old legends talk about a landmark called the Big Toe. We think we are near it, but I don't know if it's north or south of us. The passageway was dug a long time ago, but there should still be evidence of it. Our miners will find it."

"We could set up a base here and look in both directions," suggested Weevil. "Chomp will take half the gnomes, and I'll take the other half."

"No time to make a camp," answered Ludicra. "Filbum and I will go with you, and Crawfleece can go with Captain Chomp. How will we let the other group know when we've found it?"

"We'll shoot fire arrows into the sky," answered Chomp. "So keep somebody on watch." He pointed to a handful of gnomes and growled, "You five with me!"

"Uh, when do we eat?" asked Gnat, stepping close enough to Weevil to let everyone know that he was going with her.

"On the march," answered Chomp.

"It will be a slow march, because we've got to search every inch as we go," said Gnat. "Light your hats!"

With much ceremony, the gnomes lit the oil lanterns in their helmets and checked their tools. Like fireflies rising from a meadow, ten dots of light spread along the black river of nothingness. Gradually the darkness swallowed the dots, until nothing was seen or heard except for the soft chattering of the gnomes.

The troop of elves dragged Rollo into a quiet village of leaf huts and low tree houses, lit only by a few torches. No one was around, which surprised the troll until he remembered that elves slept at night and lived by daylight. *How weird,* he thought. They took him to the gazebo in the center of the village and dumped him there, his hands and legs still tied up. He looked around and remembered a feast he had eaten in this gazebo, or one just like it. His visit with Stygius Rex and General Drool now seemed like years ago, but it had been only a few weeks.

The party of elves didn't wake everyone in the village; they were quiet, merely whispering to each other. Rollo wondered whether this was even *their* village, because it took them a while to locate the one they had come to see. Rollo's head hurt from all the bumping around, but he remembered a name with a title . . . Melinda, the Enchantress Mother.

Finally the red-bearded elf named Prince Thatch climbed the steps of the gazebo, an elder female clinging to his arm. This elf had bone-white hair that hung to the ground, and her face was as wrinkled as an ogre's underarm. Yet she wore a white gown that was as silky and pale as fairy wings.

Upon seeing Rollo, Melinda scowled in disgust, and the troll lost heart. Then she motioned wildly to Prince Thatch and ordered, "Untie him. This is not how we treat guests!"

"He is not a guest," answered Thatch with a sneer. "Besides, he can fly."

"So he returned of his own will," answered the elder elf. "By himself. Where is the box and knife of which you spoke?"

"Here, Enchantress Mother." The prince snapped his fingers, and his underling, Filch, approached them carrying the tiny coffin and the black knife. He placed them reverently into the spotted hands of the old female, and her eyes widened with shock upon touching them.

"There is great magic in these items," she said. "And you looked inside the box?"

Thatch nodded sheepishly. "We all did. It's Clipper all right. . . . She looks like she's sleeping, not dead."

Showing surprising strength, the Enchantress Mother bent down and used the black knife to cut Rollo's bonds. As he had seen, the strands melted at the knife's touch. "Stand up," said the elder. "And Filch, go into my cellar and get him something to eat and drink."

Looking doubtful, the blond-haired elf hurried away, and Rollo breathed a sigh of relief. "Thank you," he rasped as he staggered to his feet. "I never meant you any harm . . . not before and not on this visit."

"Your name is?"

"Rollo."

The elder nodded. "And you won't fly away?"

"No," he insisted. "I want to help you bring Clipper back to life, if I can."

"Have you ever seen this knife used in such a fashion?" asked Melinda.

Rollo shook his head glumly. "No, but I know it has power."

"Oh, I know that too," agreed the Enchantress Mother. She hefted the serpent knife in a trembling hand. "Just what *kind* of power is the question. It's very old—I can feel the weight of ages in this weapon. And it's sharp."

40

"It saved my life," said Rollo. "But Stygius Rex was known to make ghouls with it."

"So . . . does it do good for good folk, and bad for bad folk?" The Enchantress Mother shook her head and looked at the tiny coffin in her other hand. "And what will it do to a poor fairy who only wanted to make a new friend?"

"I don't know," admitted Rollo. He sniffed the scent of food on the wind and turned his gaze to the blond-haired elf, who came bearing a basket of fruit, bread, and greens. He also had a skin full of water.

Filch dropped the food in front of Rollo as if he were a wild animal, and the troll fell upon it. He gobbled loudly, not caring what the elves thought of his table manners. *Let them hang in a spiderweb for a week without eating, and then see how they treat food.* He had never tasted fruit this huge and sweet, so unlike the bitter berries of the swamp, and he licked the juice off his fur.

"You eat and rest, young troll," said the kindly Mother Enchantress. "I want to study these objects and think about what we should do. Prince Thatch, I will hold you responsible if any harm befalls him."

"Yes, Mother Enchantress," replied the elf with a courtly bow. When the elder was gone, Thatch glared at the feasting troll. "You remember to behave yourself, or an accident might happen to you."

"You know," burped Rollo, his mouth stuffed with fruit,

"I don't blame you for being mad at us. But your real quarrel is with only one Bonespittlian, who is gone."

"Are you sure the vaunted sorcerer Stygius Rex is dead?" asked Thatch.

Rollo shrugged his big shoulders. "I fought with him in the Rawchill River—after he killed Clipper—and I think he drowned. We haven't found his body, no. But if Stygius Rex were alive, I wouldn't be here talking calmly to you. He'd be after me."

"I see," answered the elf, stroking his red beard thoughtfully. He narrowed blazing blue eyes at Rollo and asked, "Who do you side with in this war between the fairies and the birds?"

Rollo shook his head puzzledly. "I remember a talking parrot when I was last here. . . . That's all I know about it."

"Ah, yes, Kendo," said Thatch scornfully. "I knew he must have had something to do with the war. This sorcerer of yours was very evil."

"And that was one of his *good* traits," answered Rollo.

Prince Thatch scowled and strode down the steps of the gazebo. He surveyed the sleeping elven village, then motioned to his archers, who surrounded Rollo with their arrows cocked upon their bowstrings. *They don't know trolls very well,* thought Rollo, *because I'm not going anywhere while they're feeding me such good food.*

As Ludicra, Weevil, Filbum, and their half of the gnomes searched the rim of the Great Chasm, weariness slowed their every step. Plus the gnomes were annoying in the way they peered under every rock and poked into every crevice. Though Ludicra supposed it was necessary to be thorough, the delays drove her crazy. They were all tired from traveling without sleep, but trolls were used to getting little sleep.

"Come on," she complained, "there's nothing here. Let's keep moving."

Gnat yawned at her and motioned to his miners to keep looking. Their little headlamps bobbed across the rocky terrain as he explained, "You must understand, Ludicra, we know how to look for burrows, and you don't."

The would-be queen sniffed. "Where do you think trolls live? In tree houses?"

"Hey!" called Weevil, pointing into the night sky. "There's something odd coming across the chasm."

"Coming across?" asked the troll. She followed the ogre's outstretched talon and saw what looked like a black cloud floating over the emptiness of the gorge. Ludicra started to tell the others to take cover, but she saw that the gnomes were already hidden. Weevil and Filbum drew their clubs and backed away from the approaching apparition.

Something else caught Ludicra's eye, and she saw a similar cloud emerge from the Bonny Woods farther down the canyon. As this second cloud soared across the chasm, the first cloud changed course and swerved to meet it. The trolls and ogres watched in amazement as the two ominous blotches moved toward each other, like a thunderstorm building. It looked as if they would meet near the spot where Ludicra's small band was perched on the rim.

"What are they?" asked Filbum. "Bats?"

"That would be my guess," said Weevil.

Ludicra shook her head. "We don't know if they have bats in the Bonny Woods, but we know they have fairies."

"Fairies!" exclaimed Filbum with fear. The young troll stumbled over his own feet as he retreated from the rim.

"Steady there," said Weevil. "They're not after us."

"Yet," answered Ludicra with a shiver.

Now they could hear a faint squawking from the flock on the left—it sure didn't sound like bats. From the second cloud came a soft chattering, almost like the voices of children. They didn't sound like bats either.

"Get down," said Weevil, crouching in the rugged terrain. Ludicra and Filbum were quick to follow her suggestion.

They watched in awe as the two great flocks plowed into each other like two attacking armies. The dark sky erupted with horrendous screeching and shrieking, the shapes a blur as they swirled and careened into each other. It was not a friendly meeting, and some of the winged creatures plummeted from the sky into the nothingness of the canyon.

Furious fluttering sounded, and a large green creature with a beak, wings, talons, and feathers landed at Ludicra's feet. The flier stared at them in confusion for a moment. When Weevil reached for the flier, it pecked at her hand. Flapping its wings in panic, the creature managed to lift itself off the ground and rejoin the battle.

"Do you think that could be a bird?" asked Weevil.

"Birds are all black," answered Filbum. "Not green, like fresh slime."

"Maybe birds are green in the Bonny Woods," suggested Ludicra.

Filbum frowned doubtfully. "Green birds?"

Two combatants suddenly swerved over their heads, and the visitors ducked for cover. Still, Ludicra managed to watch in amazement as a brilliant blue bird battled with a white creature that had arms, legs, and a head to go with its wings. They were about the same size, and the bird used its beak and talons, while the white being wielded tiny blades. Both of them got in a few blows, then darted off.

Filbum shivered. "Was that—?"

"Yes, it was a fairy," answered Weevil with a grimace. "Cute things, aren't they?"

Ludicra suddenly sneezed, and rubbed her nose. Soon the three visitors were sneezing uncontrollably. They could hear the hidden gnomes sneezing too.

Weevil sniffed. "Let's retreat—achoo!—until the battle is over."

By the time they moved back from the rim and stopped sneezing, the furious flocks had departed from the chasm. The melee was over, but the whole thing had been disturbing to Ludicra. It was supposed to be pleasant and peaceful in the Bonny Woods, not full of battles and sneezing fits.

More than ever, Ludicra knew they had to find Rollo as quickly as possible.

"Gnomes, on your feet!" she shouted. "Let's find that tunnel!"

Still sniffling their runny noses, the gnomes crawled out of their hiding places and lit their lanterns. Gnat made sure they went back to the last place they had looked, and once again they were turning over rocks and peering into gopher holes. An hour later, Ludicra, impatient with their methodical pace, began to stomp around.

"Come on!" she whined. "Let's move faster. At this rate, it will take all our lifetimes to search this canyon!"

Gnat glared at her. "You don't want us to miss it, do you?"

"Bonespittle is falling apart!" she shouted. "In the Bonny Woods, flying creatures darken the sky, battling each other. Both lands are in dire need of a king to bring us peace, and *we* are the only hope. We can't miss finding it, because we can't *afford* to fail!"

As her furry, taloned feet stomped the ground, the sand broke beneath her, and Ludicra dropped into thin air. She screamed as she plummeted downward, thinking she would fall forever. But the drop ended as quickly as it had begun, and her plump rear landed hard on subterranean rock. The wind knocked out of her, Ludicra gasped for breath. As she wheezed, she looked around her dank surroundings. It was mostly dirt and darkness, but the rock beneath the fallen dirt felt smooth. A strange draft of stale air whistled past her bulbous nose.

A second later, five lantern lights peered over the edge of the hole into which she had fallen. By the wobbly beams, Ludicra saw that she had made the cavity with her angry stomping, and that the bottom of it was unnaturally smooth. She wasn't in a pit but in the middle of an underground passageway, which stretched into darkness in both directions.

"You found it!" said Gnat with a gasp.

Looking down at her, Weevil laughed. "Do you suppose that's what they meant by the 'Big Toe'?"

Ludicra staggered to her feet and rubbed her sore behind. "Send up the fire arrow!"

"At once," responded Weevil, drawing her bow. "Gnat, if I may have some fire, please."

"Certainly," he answered, taking the lid off his helmet lantern. "Now do you think we can stop to rest?"

"All right," said Ludicra. Her voice echoed in the underground passageway, and she waved to the gnomes, who were already lowering their ropes; they wanted to get underground as quickly as possible. "We'll stop to rest . . . but only until Chomp gets here."

In the elven village, Rollo lay on the floor of the gazebo, burping. Empty baskets were strewn all around him. His stomach was full like it had never been before, and he felt contented. If he had to die now, he mused, it would be a tragedy, but a happy one. The elves watched him with disgust, and the blond one, Filch, said, "Do all trolls eat like that?"

"*No* trolls eat like that," answered Rollo with a belch. "We never get a chance."

"Is it really that bad where you come from?" asked the elf. "Is that why you want to invade us?"

"We don't want to invade you," answered Rollo, rolling onto his side. "Well, one of us did, but he's gone. The trolls thought we were going to build a bridge across the Great Chasm, so we could all become friends."

The elves laughed at this naive notion. "Friends with trolls, ogres, and ghouls?" asked Filch in amazement.

"Uh, we don't have ghouls anymore," answered Rollo. "And we're just as afraid of elves and fairies as you are of us."

That brought a scowl to the elf's face. "The idea of a bridge across the Great Chasm is ridiculous."

"So is the idea of a flying troll," answered Rollo, "but here I am." He glanced upward to see a hint of redness glimmering through the treetops. "Is daylight coming?"

"Soon," answered Filch. "You fear daylight, don't you?"

Rollo shrugged. "I've always liked it, but that is normally when we sleep." The big troll yawned and slumped across the crude planks of the gazebo. "So, good day!"

The troll's loud snoring roared across the elven village in the early morning hours, and several children gathered around the gazebo. After overcoming their initial fear, the young elves watched him curiously. The guards warned them to stay back, but it was clear that Rollo wasn't going to harm anything except the morning peace. The children giggled at his big hairy feet, batwing ears, and warty nose. Vaguely, Rollo heard them through his dreams, which were about eating, and it made him smile even wider.

When they stirred him awake, the sun was so high in the sky that it twinkled through the roof slats of the gazebo. "Come on, troll," said Prince Thatch. "You don't need to sleep the whole day. We're ready."

Rollo blinked at the gruff, red-bearded elf. "Ready for what?" he muttered.

The elf scowled darkly: "To resurrect your little friend. But I warn you, troll, if this is some kind of evil trick, I've got a poison arrow just for you."

The troll scrunched his face with distaste but managed to keep his temper. "I just wanted to bring Clipper home, but if we can do more for her—"

"Come along then," snapped the elf. "We have some distance to walk . . . to a special place."

Rollo burped. "What about breakfast?"

Prince Thatch growled and waved for the troll to follow him into the lush, emerald forest.

CHAPTER 5

HAPPY TRAILS TO YOU

ONCE THEY GOT UNDERGROUND IN THE COLD, DARK tunnel on the edge of the Great Chasm, everyone in Ludicra's party was much happier. It was a perfectly hideous place—dripping, oozing, smelly, slimy—but quite spacious. Even the trolls and ogres could walk upright without banging their heads. The gnomes inspected every inch of the sloping passageway as they descended, and they discussed every gooey crack and crevice.

Ludicra caught up with Gnat in order to hear their conversation. "This tunnel is in good shape," she said. "How old do you suppose it is?"

The young gnome looked up at her thoughtfully. "Old . . . very old. From before the sorcerers took over Bonespittle, I would say. Gnomes didn't build this place, you know."

"They didn't?" asked Ludicra, surprised.

"No, it's too big," answered Gnat. "Gnomes don't need all this headroom." He motioned into the wide-open spaces above his head.

"More rats!" shouted Crawfleece gleefully as she plodded past them, with Filbum and the ogres right behind her. Thuds, whacks, and horrified squeaks echoed throughout the sloping tunnel as the travelers picked up a little snack.

"Then who did build it?" asked Ludicra.

"You tell me," answered Gnat. "Do you recognize any of the handiwork?"

Ludicra gaped at him. "You think trolls built it?"

Gnat lowered his voice to say, "Well, I've never seen ogres build anything. They can put up tents, and that's about it. My uncle Runt told me that trolls were once the rulers of Bonespittle. Of course, I think he heard that from Rollo."

"Rollo," said Ludicra wistfully. "Do you think he's all right?"

"Anyone who can vanquish Stygius Rex and all his ghouls can take care of himself," answered Gnat. "What do you think?"

Ludicra shrugged her chubby shoulders, but said nothing. Now that they were on their way to the bottom of the Great Chasm, she had hope that they could reach him in time. She didn't know how she knew it, but Ludicra could sense that Rollo was in grave danger. After all, she wasn't there to advise him. . . .

Gnat went on, "Although it hasn't been recent, somebody has done some maintenance here."

"Maintenance?" asked the young troll.

Gnat looked around and saw two of his fellow gnomes inspecting a dark slab of mortar on the cavern wall. By herself, Ludicra never would have noticed it. "See there," said Gnat, pointing to the spot. "A repair to fix water damage."

Ludicra frowned in thought. "But who—"

"Stairs!" shouted Crawfleece ahead of them. "We found stairs going down!"

The gnomes hurried forward, chattering excitedly amongst themselves. Gnat turned to Ludicra and shrugged. "I expected we would find stairs. After all, we were never going to get to the bottom at this easy incline."

"No, I guess not," said Ludicra, thinking Gnat was pretty smart.

The party halted at the first fork they found in the tunnel. A crude stairwell led down into pitch darkness, while the passageway continued onward, sloping upward. At this junction, there was also a small chamber carved into the rock, and inside it lay a pile of moss-covered bones, scattered about as if left over from a feast.

"It looks like a guard post," said Captain Chomp, peering into the chamber.

"To guard against what?" asked Filbum. "Nobody knows about this place, do they?"

"They do now," answered Chomp, hefting his club and

an oil lantern. "Anybody object if I go first?"

"Be my guest," said Weevil with a smile. "I'll bring up the rear. Let's keep together—no stragglers."

It was a cheerful, energized band that clomped down the damp steps. Beautiful slime and mold grew on the oozing stone walls, and the whole place smelled like a ghoul's underarm. The gnomes began to sing a marching tune in a minor key; the trolls joined in, while the ogres bared their tusks and hummed along.

The solemn band of elves—and one troll—plodded single file through the overgrown forest. Archers kept watch on the trees, probably for birds, thought Rollo. The Enchantress Mother, Melinda, was closely guarded in the center of the line. She carried Clipper's coffin and the black serpent knife in a net bag clutched to her chest. Prince Thatch and his servant, Filch, kept watch on Rollo at the end of the file.

It was strange to be walking in the Bonny Woods without hearing the cheerful call of birds or the fluttering of fairies. But they were off by themselves, thought Rollo, waging their own battles.

"Prince Thatch," said the troll, "are you going to tell the fairies what we're doing?"

"No need," answered the red-bearded elf. He motioned around at the thick trees and overgrown path. "They're watching us now. They always watch."

Rollo glanced around nervously, but he couldn't see any

53

small, winged beings hidden in the underbrush. Of course, that was the point.

The path wound upward toward one of the tors, or tall hills, that dotted the Bonny Woods. Rollo shivered, because he had been stuck in a spider's web in one of those same rugged outcroppings of rock. This one was decorated with red and green pennants, and elves were stationed on various ledges, waiting for them. In due time, they marched into a clearing, where a circle of small rocks surrounded a large boulder. On the boulder were smudge marks and crude vessels full of water. *It looks like a holy place with an altar,* thought Rollo.

Reverently, the elves filed into the clearing and took their places around the circle. The Enchantress Mother went to the boulder in the center and carefully placed the box and knife on the altar. She motioned to Rollo to join her, and Prince Thatch shoved him forward.

Sheepishly the hulking troll took his place beside the elder elf, and she gave him an encouraging smile. "Don't be nervous," she whispered, "although *I* am."

This was the first time Rollo had spoken to Melinda since they had dragged him into the village. He gulped and said, "Do you think it will work?"

"I have consulted the knuckle bones and emu feathers," answered Melinda. "They say that today there is magic in the air. If we fail, it just means we still have a dead fairy, right?"

Rollo nodded.

"Stand behind me," ordered Melinda, "and steady me if I start to falter. We must form a circle of protection."

The troll nodded again and took his place behind the wizened elf. She lifted her hands, and the elves grew quiet and riveted their attention on the Enchantress Mother. Melinda began to chant in a surprisingly low voice, like an ogre snoring, and the elves linked hands and began to sway. Most of the elves had their eyes closed, except for those on the tor, who remained on guard. The fairies rose from the forest like the mist.

These ethereal beings flew into the air and formed a circle around the elven circle, and their voices twittered like children at play. Everyone was chanting and swaying, with arms linked, and it was so wholesome that it made Rollo's fur crawl. Perhaps there really was magic in the air, because the whole forest seemed to shimmer around them.

With trembling hands, Melinda opened the coffinwood box and took out Clipper's limp body. The fairy appeared to be an especially exquisite doll, and the elf laid her gently on the altar. When she picked up the black knife with the serpent handle, both her hands began to shake. Melinda looked helplessly at Rollo, and he mimed stabbing it into Clipper's body. He couldn't figure out another way to do it, although it seemed cruel to stab that beautiful body, even if it was lifeless.

As the Enchantress Mother lowered the knife to Clipper's body, it glowed with a sickly green light. The radiant weapon writhed in her hands like a living snake, and Melinda gasped and almost dropped it. Quickly Rollo wrapped his arms around her slender body and cupped her hands with his. Together they were able to force the shimmering, twisting blade toward Clipper's body.

Melinda was weak, and Rollo had to supply the strength needed to pierce the fairy's chest. As the knife drew a single drop of black blood, the fairy twitched as if stung. Then she opened her eyes and stared at them, and the chanting of the elves and fairies became frenzied.

There was indeed magic in the air, because the fairy suddenly sprang to life. Clipper jumped to her feet, spread her wings, and fluttered into the air. Rollo gasped, for her wing had been broken when she was last alive. But it was broken no more—the magical knife seemed to have cured all her ills. With joy and confusion, the small fairy darted about, then her eyes hit upon the troll's wide orbs.

"Rollo!" she called with delight. "Rollo, what is this?"

"You're alive!" he shouted happily.

Before he could say anything more, Clipper was surrounded by joyful fairies, tugging on her hands, feet, and wings. They laughed and flitted about, and the elves shook off their amazement and cheered. A moment later, Rollo was surrounded by elves and fairies, all shaking his talons and slapping him on his hairy back. Melinda even hugged him, and soon a dozen elves were hugging him.

While all this was going on, Rollo kept his eyes on one

thing: the snake knife. He didn't want to lose that knife. He reached for the dark blade a moment before Prince Thatch had the same idea. The red-haired elf glared at him for a moment, then he smiled broadly and slapped the troll on the back. The delirious elves tried to pick him up and carry him off in triumph, but no amount of elves could lift the big troll.

Somehow Rollo managed to return the black knife to the sheath on his belt. The chaos in the sacred clearing continued until Prince Thatch had a wonderful idea.

"Let's have a feast!" shouted the leader. "Back to the village!"

The crowd roared with agreement, and soon all of them were romping and skipping through the forest. With the promise of food, Rollo was in the lead, but it was hard to run with fairies dropping upon his head to kiss and touch him. "Hail Rollo!" they shouted over and over again.

Rollo felt a tug on his floppy ear, and a small figure landed upon his shoulder in a familiar place. He turned to see Clipper, her eyes glistening with tears. She smiled and said, "Thank you, Rollo. You brought me home."

"Do you feel all right?" he asked with concern.

"Never felt better!" answered the fairy cheerfully. "You used the black knife?"

"Yes, and I was a little worried," he admitted.

"About *me?*" Clipper gave him a twinkling laugh. "I'm used to magic. Tell me what happened. What became of Stygius Rex?"

"He drowned in the river, but we never found his body."

"And Bonespittle?"

Rollo shrugged his beefy shoulders. "They wanted to make me king, but I had to come here with you first."

Clipper grinned and clapped her hands. "So Bonespittle is free! The trolls are free. It was a happy ending?"

"Except for you dying," answered Rollo. Although he used to see ghouls all the time, it was still strange talking to a being who had recently been expired. "Are you sure you feel all right?"

She pinched his ear. "Don't worry so much about me, Rollo. Being dead is like . . . sleeping too long after a big meal. That's what you're going to do, right?"

Rollo laughed. "Yes, I am."

"I have to see my friends and family," said Clipper, fluttering into the air. "I'll meet you at the feast!"

"Right!" he answered. He turned to wave, but she was already gone, joining a huge flock of chattering fairies.

"Giant snail!" called Crawfleece. She and Filbum pushed past Captain Chomp and bounded down the stairs toward a large shelled creature spreading slime across the ceiling. Both of them were already drooling with anticipation of fresh snail meat.

"Slow down!" called Ludicra. She wanted Chomp and the gnomes to go first, because they had the light and were more cautious. But it was too late. Just as Crawfleece and

Filbum reached the fleeing mollusk, several stairs disappeared beneath them, and they dropped from sight.

"Look out!" warned Chomp. The big ogre spread his arms and kept the others from running headlong into the pit. "It's a trap! These stairs are trapped—everyone hold still!"

The party bunched up in a collision on the steps, pushing Chomp forward. By sheer strength, the ogre managed to skid to a stop before he followed the trolls into the hole. "Hold still!" he bellowed. Meanwhile, the big snail slithered away, unharmed.

"We're trying," said Ludicra. "Where did they go?"

Chomp shrugged doubtfully and peered into the blackness before him. "Help!" squeaked a frightened voice from the depths. A couple of claws were visible, digging into the last step before the drop, and Chomp reached down to grab one. Grunting with the effort, he managed to pull Filbum partly out.

"Troll, you eat too much!" growled Chomp. "You are heavy!"

"That's because Crawfleece is hanging on to my feet," muttered the young troll.

"Help him!" Weevil muscled her way through the crowd and managed to grab Filbum's other claw. The gnomes chattered worriedly and tried to hide. Ludicra wanted to help, but she was still obeying Chomp's order to not move. Old habits—with the ogres being the bosses—were hard to break.

With considerable effort, the ogres managed to drag

Filbum and Crawfleece out of the revealed pit. For several minutes, they all lay panting on the stairs. Ludicra moved forward with a lantern and shined the light into the square hole. Although the beams went down twenty feet, she still couldn't see the bottom.

"You two were lucky," she told Crawfleece and Filbum. "Next time, don't let your stomachs overrule your brains."

"How do we get across?" asked Gnat worriedly.

Ludicra was about to reply that they could jump across, but then she realized the gnomes were too small for that. "We'll have to test the stairs on the other side," she answered. "In fact, we'll have to test all the stairs as we go. With a long enough pole, that will be easy . . . but slow."

"What kind of fiends would build a trap like that?" grumbled Crawfleece.

"Trolls," answered Ludicra. "I noticed a counterweight system and a span lock, like the kind we use. This trap is basically a collapsible bridge. We'll probably push a step farther down that will close it."

"That's amazing," said Filbum. "Hey, where did that snail go?"

"Forget the snail," said Ludicra. "Let's get moving, but slowly. We'll tie two clubs together to make a pole, and the gnomes will go first."

"Why should the gnomes go first?" protested Gnat.

"Because they're lighter," answered Ludicra. "And we can throw you across this hole."

Gnat scowled. "*Throw* us across? That sounds dangerous."

Ludicra shook her head. "I thought you were looking for adventure. Well, you found it."

Gnat gulped and looked back at his fellow gnomes. Minutes later, the band was again descending the stairs . . . but slowly. The gnomes carefully tapped each step with a pole before they walked on it. All of them were still enjoying the cool, slimy tunnel, and they had new respect for the builders.

Realizing that they needed their wits about them, Ludicra gave the band permission to sleep for a few hours. As she lay on a hard step, trying to get comfortable, she wondered what Rollo was doing. Was he suffering? Was he in danger?

Why do I care so much? she wondered. *Rollo is just a means to my becoming queen, the first queen of Bonespittle.* But a queen wasn't much good without a king.

"Buuurrp!" belched Rollo as he pushed himself away from the table, rolled off the log, and fell to the ground. Elves and fairies gathered around him and hooted with laughter, because they had never seen a troll eat himself silly. Rollo had never seen a troll eat so much either, because there was never enough food in the Dismal Swamp to eat like this.

There was still plenty of exotic food on the banquet table—fruits, nuts, mushrooms, vegetables, roast fowl, bread and rolls, and sumptuous desserts made with honey. Every few minutes, it seemed, the cooks brought out more trays of food! Rollo couldn't believe he was giving up, but he was finished. Night had fallen hours ago, and more elves and fairies were arriving from other villages to partake in the feast. It looked as if the celebration might go on for days.

"Had enough?" whispered an amused voice in his ear.

With effort, Rollo turned his head to see a chuckling fairy. At his pained expression, Clipper doubled over with laughter. Then she jumped onto his bulging stomach and rubbed it gently. "Poor troll, you need to rest now. Let somebody else take over the eating chores. Let's get you to a hut."

The fairy rounded up half a dozen elves, who helped the stuffed troll to his feet. Everything was a blur as he staggered into the nearest hut and collapsed. Clipper thanked the elves and dropped down to hover near Rollo's ear.

"I've got to go stand watch against the birds, but you sleep," she cooed. "You deserve to rest, after all you've done."

With a belch, Rollo nodded and closed his eyes. Instinctively, his hand reached for the black knife in his belt, and he found it there, nestled safely in its sheath.

"Good night, Clipper," he said with a satisfied smile.

"Good night, my friend," answered the beautiful fairy.

When Rollo awoke, daylight was streaming through the doorway of the hut. He rubbed his eyes and rolled over. His stomach still felt as if he had drunk half of Dismal Swamp, but he managed to stagger to his feet. Rollo could hear laughter and chatter outside, and he knew the feast was still in full swing. *Well, maybe I have room for lunch,* he thought.

As he walked toward the door, the troll reached for the handle of the black knife—but the sheath was empty. The serpent knife was gone!

Rollo got down on his knees and combed the earthen floor of the hut, but the knife wasn't there. He'd had it when he went to sleep last night, he was sure. But it was gone now.

Somebody must have stolen it! But who?

The troll lumbered out the door into the middle of the village. Festivities were still in progress, and there were more elves and fairies than last night. Or so it seemed. Rollo looked around for Prince Thatch, who had tried to grab the knife yesterday. He found the elven leader sitting at the head of the banquet table, toasting with honey wine.

"Hello, Rollo!" called Prince Thatch. "We were just saluting your good health!"

"Did you take it?" asked Rollo angrily.

"Take what?" replied the elf, his smile fading.

Suddenly Rollo knew he had made a mistake, but it was too late now. "The black knife—it's gone."

Prince Thatch leaped to his feet, his bearded face a frozen mask of anger. "If this is a trick—"

"No trick," answered Rollo glumly. "It was stolen while I slept. Anyone could have gone into that hut."

A hand touched his arm, and Rollo turned to see

Melinda, the Enchantress Mother. "This is very serious," she said with a grave frown. "Who would want that knife?"

He shrugged. "Well, someone who wanted to bring the dead back to life, I guess." Through the fuzziness of his sleepy brain, Rollo feared that he knew the answer to Melinda's question. "Where is Clipper?"

"Why do you seek the fairy?" asked the wizened elf.

"Clipper!" called the troll.

"Clipper!" demanded Prince Thatch, suddenly getting worried. He gazed at a handful of fairies gathered at the table. "What has become of Clipper?"

"We don't know!" squeaked the fairies in fear.

"Find her!" roared the elf.

At once, the fairies darted into the sky. Within a few seconds, a large flock of them hovered over the treetops, flying back and forth like a confused cloud. Rollo had a sinking feeling in his stomach as he watched the fey folk search in vain for their missing member. For what seemed like forever, cries of "Clipper!" echoed throughout the forest.

When they returned to the ground, Rollo steeled himself for the bad news. "Clipper is gone," reported an elder fairy. "No one has seen her since last night."

Now every eye in the village turned toward Rollo, and they were all angry, suspicious eyes. Prince Thatch drew an arrow and knocked it against his bow. "I said I had a poison arrow for you if you betrayed us."

"Wait!" begged Rollo. "I didn't know what she would do! We still don't know for sure."

The Mother Enchantress moved to lower Thatch's deadly arrow. "If this were Rollo's plot, he would have escaped too."

"Perhaps he's a dumb plotter," answered the red-bearded elf. "Take him prisoner until we learn what has happened. Don't try to fly, or you'll get a dozen arrows before you reach the trees."

"I won't," muttered Rollo. As elves and fairies surrounded him, the young troll lowered his shaggy head. Maybe he should just take the poison arrow in the chest right now, he thought, because he deserved it. Thatch was right—he was incredibly dumb to have used that cursed knife on anyone. It was the same knife Stygius Rex had used to create the ghouls.

Sure, it brought the dead back to life, but what else did it do to them?

CHAPTER 6

THE EVIL DEAD

CLIPPER HOVERED OVER THE RAWCHILL RIVER, GAZING into the icy water with intent eyes. Snagged on a large branch under the freezing rapids lay the body of Stygius Rex. His black robes flowed in the rushing current, and the sorcerer's jagged face looked peaceful, if pale with cold and death. In the fairy's hands was the black knife, and it was nearly as big as she. Now that the weapon had found its master, it glowed with a sickly green aura.

Clipper beat her wings fiercely, trying to stay aloft with the heavy weapon. She wasn't exactly sure what she was supposed to do. Even though the serpent knife had been employed on her, she had never seen it used. The fairy glanced at the black wound on her white chest, and she suddenly knew what she had to do.

She plunged into the river, the dagger pointed forward. As soon as the blade struck the dead sorcerer, his eyes sprang open, and he grabbed her. Flying effortlessly, Stygius Rex lifted both of them out of the frigid river and floated toward the bank. They landed safely on the ground, and the sorcerer shook himself dry like a big dog.

Gently he took the knife from the demented fairy and set her in the mud. "Ah, my trusty knife has saved me again!" crowed Stygius Rex. He returned the weapon to his belt and shivered. "I hate being dead."

"Me too," muttered Clipper. "Welcome home!"

The sorcerer smiled malevolently. "And I have a new ally. Did that fool use the knife on you?"

"Yes, master," answered Clipper with a regal curtsy.

Stygius Rex roared with laughter. "I think Rollo is as much enchanted by this knife as we are. I guess he didn't realize that it would turn you bad."

"No, master," said Clipper with a chuckle. "I stole it from him as he slept."

"Fine job, little one," answered Stygius Rex. "I was already wonderfully evil, and now I'll be more evil than ever!"

Clipper clapped her tiny hands with joy. "Bravo, master!"

"So what has happened in Bonespittle and the Bonny Woods?"

The fairy shrugged. "I don't know much—I was dead until just yesterday. Rollo told me that they wanted to make him king of Bonespittle."

The sorcerer grimaced with disgust. "That meddling fool! So he thought he could get my job, did he? *Over my dead body!*"

They both laughed at the unexpected joke. Stygius Rex stroked his warty chin and gazed down at the wet fairy. "I've lost all my ghouls, but I've gained a henchfairy."

"Yes, master," said Clipper brightly. "Perhaps my sneezing and itching spells will be stronger than ever."

"One can hope," responded the sorcerer. "At least I have an ally who can fly by herself. And one who will remain loyal to me. You will be loyal, won't you?"

"We are united in evil," answered the demented fairy with a wicked gleam in her eye.

"Then come, Henchfairy," said Stygius Rex, rising into the gloomy sky over the Rawchill River. "We have much to do."

"What is *this?*" asked Ludicra in amazement. She and the rest of the trolls, ogres, and gnomes stood before a great cavern full of toppled pillars and broken statues. By the light of their flickering lanterns, they couldn't see more than a small part of the ruins, but it looked like a courtyard from a great city made of stone. It was hard to tell what creatures had inhabited this place, because no one in Bonespittle lived like this. Ludicra had never seen a stone city, even underground.

Although the statues lay in pieces, they didn't seem to

represent creatures with two legs and two arms. The beings honored by these statues had long tails and wings, or so it seemed from the fragments on the floor. The floor itself was amazing—an intricate mosaic pattern that must have been beautiful at one time. Now it was covered by the dust and debris of ages unknown.

Her square jaw hanging open, Ludicra stepped into the ruined city.

"Be careful!" warned Chomp. "It might be another trap."

As she halted, Ludicra heard rustling in the shadows ahead of her. She caught a glimpse of something slithering through the debris; it was large and green, with spines on its back. The gnomes disappeared, and everyone retreated, except for Crawfleece, who edged forward.

"That looks like lunch to me," said the brawny troll.

"Crawfleece," whispered Ludicra, "that beast looked like it was a good twenty feet long."

The troll licked her blue lips. "Enough for everybody!"

Weevil stepped forward and said, "I don't see a way to go around. We'll probably have to go through here to find the stairs down."

"Stick close together," ordered Chomp, hefting his club. The big ogre looked around and scowled. "Somebody find the gnomes!"

From the shadowy ruins came a hissing sound, and the ogres and trolls dropped into fighting stances. Ludicra had missed the combat training at the Rawchill River, so she slipped behind Crawfleece, as did Filbum. That move wasn't a moment too soon, because a humongous beast that looked like a cross between a lizard and a catfish sprang from the ruins. It grabbed the nearest ogre and swallowed him whole, before Weevil, Chomp, and the rest of them fell upon it with their clubs and blades.

The thing thrashed in agony and anger, but its whiskered mouth was already full. As it tried to slither away, the growling ogres bashed it with dreadful glee. Crawfleece joined in, attempting to cut off a chunk of the thing's tail. It seemed to have thick, scaly skin, like a snapper, and Ludicra wondered if there was a swamp nearby. Whacking and whomping the monster, the ogres chased it into the court-yard of fallen pillars, where it tried to seek refuge.

"Gnat!" shouted Ludicra. "Get your gnomes out here! Clear some room."

Reluctantly, but with the drool of hunger on their lips, the gnomes emerged to join in the chase. Though they didn't fight, they pushed away enough of the debris to let the war-riors reach the beast. The battle was going well, even with the loss of one of their number, until another hissing sound echoed from the rear of the huge cavern. Nobody else seemed to notice, so busy were they with the slaughter, but Ludicra heard sloshing sounds from the depths of the chamber.

She maneuvered around the battle to follow the sound, and she saw a shimmering pool in the center of a broken ring of pillars. Suddenly Ludicra could envision this place as it had existed in the past—a temple to some archaic deity. And that deity was lumbering out of the pool as she stared wide-eyed at it. This creature was just like the other one—a fishy, reptilian thing with enormous spines—only it was five times bigger.

The whooping and hollering behind her told Ludicra that the band had claimed victory over the smaller beast. "Can we cut Rondu out?" asked Chomp, looking into the mouth of the vanquished beast for his missing ogre.

"Build a fire!" shouted Crawfleece. "Let's have roasted . . . whatever-it-is!"

"What a great place this is!" hooted Gnat. "I'd like to stay down here forever!"

"Um, comrades—," said Ludicra, backing toward them. "I'd like you to see something."

"Not now," said Crawfleece, "we're busy. Captain Chomp, I'll need your big sword to fillet this fish."

"You'll need a bigger sword than that," replied Ludicra with a gulp. She grabbed Crawfleece by her hairy shoulders and spun her around to face the approaching behemoth. The big troll's eyes grew even bigger than her appetite.

"Whoa!" exclaimed Crawfleece. "That's breakfast, lunch, *and* dinner."

Now everyone turned to face the monstrosity, which had to be a hundred feet long and thirty feet high. Fortunately, it moved slowly, with its great bulk and rudimentary, finlike limbs.

The gnomes started to disappear once more, but Ludicra quickly grabbed Gnat and hoisted him off the floor. "Oh, no you don't! You and your gnomes get around that thing and find the way down. We'll distract it."

"Yeah, while it's busy eating *us!*" said Filbum, shuddering.

Chomp, Weevil, and the ogres began to beat their clubs on the mosaic tile, at the same time challenging the beast with shouts and epithets. They said some very unkind things about the monster, and it slithered forward with increased speed. The gnomes quickly fanned out through the ruins in search of the stairway down.

The leviathan paused at the corpse of its smaller version, and Ludicra could swear she saw a flash of anger in its pale pink eyes. Weevil swiftly cocked an arrow, took aim, and pierced the creature's slimy snout. It opened its whiskered mouth and roared, which brought more pillars and statues tumbling to the floor of the cavern.

"Spread out!" ordered Chomp as he picked up a fist-size rock. "Don't let it concentrate its attack!" He hurled the missile, and it bounced off the behemoth's flank as if it were a wall of stone.

As they spread out, the thing whipped its tail around and knocked Filbum about twenty feet through the air. The little troll crashed into a pillar, which broke in two and nearly crushed him. Ludicra waved to Crawfleece, and they hurried to rescue their friend. The ogres increased their shouts and noise, trying to distract the beast. The female trolls dragged Filbum away just as the monster unleashed another swipe of its tremendous tail. It missed them by inches.

"Gnat!" cried Ludicra. "You can find that passageway anytime now!"

The leviathan rose up like a snake and was about to claim more victims when Weevil threw a lantern at it. The fiery oil splashed across the creature's head and eyes, sending it into a fit of writhing and roaring. While it was temporarily blinded, they all took the opportunity to run around the monster; it was a good thing this was a big cavern. With effort, Ludicra and Crawfleece carried Filbum on their shoulders.

The enraged beast thrashed about like a fish on dry land, and more of the ruins tumbled down. In fact, the whole cavern began to shake, and rocks plummeted from the ceiling. The ogres and trolls were forced to zig and zag to avoid being crushed, and it appeared as if none would escape alive.

"Pssst!" hissed a voice. Ludicra whirled to see Gnat waving to her with his helmet lantern. "This way!"

Nearby, Weevil dove for cover from falling rocks, and Ludicra jumped into the hole with her. "Signal the others! Shoot a fire arrow!"

The ogre nodded, lit an arrow, and sent the flame arching

toward the ceiling of the massive cave. There were shouts of recognition and much scampering of feet as the ogres, trolls, and gnomes swarmed in their direction.

Following Gnat, they ran down a narrow passageway just as tons of rock and debris collapsed from the ceiling with a mighty crash. Thick clouds of dust rose up, following them down the tunnel like an angry mob. They were all coughing fitfully, and no one could see a thing—until the ground fell away beneath them. Shrieking in horror, the entire party tumbled down a flight of stairs.

With grunts and curses, they wound up in a writhing pile at the bottom of the stairwell. A monstrous roar told them that the beast knew exactly where they had gone, and they were soon falling over themselves in mad panic. Carrying the wounded, coughing and groaning, the party scrambled down another flight of stairs. They didn't rest until the anguished roars sounded very distant, then they collapsed where they stood, panting heavily.

Nearly every member of the band was bleeding and bruised, and Ludicra did a quick head count. They still had three trolls—herself, Crawfleece, and Filbum, who was groggy but alive. They were reduced to three ogres— Chomp, Weevil, and Motley—plus nine gnomes, counting Gnat. That meant they had lost only two in their narrow escape from the stone temple.

"Can we rest here?" asked Weevil, panting. "And patch ourselves up?"

Ludicra nodded and slumped to the stairs. "Yes, we rest."

After a moment of silence, Captain Chomp croaked, "Is this fun, or what!"

They all started laughing and hooting, and it was clear that none of them had ever participated in such a rousing adventure.

CHAPTER 7
UNTAPPED DANGER

T HE MILLIPEDE ATTACK STARTED QUIETLY ENOUGH. AS Ludicra followed Chomp down the dungeon stairs, a big insect rippled over her foot. The surprise caused her to jump, because the wiggler was two feet long and two knuckles wide.

It was quite a tasty morsel, and Ludicra lunged for the creature just as Crawfleece grabbed it. Her triumphant smile turned to a grimace of horror as the nasty bug slithered up her arm, stinging her ferociously. Crawfleece flipped it into the air, and the loathsome thing landed on Chomp's back.

"Hey!" the captain cried in pain. "Ouch! Whoa! Help!" He bounded around the stairs like an ogre possessed, groping helplessly in his leather armor. The millipede was apparently in some hidden fold of Chomp's flesh, stinging him mercilessly.

When the ogre started clubbing himself in the back with great whomping strokes, Ludicra and Crawfleece rushed to restrain him. Weevil arrived a moment later, and it took all three of them to hurl the enraged ogre down upon the steps. They tried to strip off his armor to reach the millipede, but that only forced the bug deeper into his clothes.

"If I can catch that wiggler, I'll fry it with grub grease," said Crawfleece, licking her lips.

They searched, but they couldn't find the twisting insect until it crawled up Weevil's arm, stinging her madly with every step. She wailed and tried to grab the wiggler, but it was as slippery as eel guts. The beast slithered into her boot, drawing more dreadful howls from the ogre. Weevil bounded one-legged down the stairs, then tumbled into the darkness with several awful thuds.

Ludicra heard shrieks and cries behind her, and she whirled to see an awful sight. Every gnome was afflicted with millipedes, crawling through their fur and clothing and around their bulbous heads. So many of the insects were pouring down the stairwell that the steps seemed to ripple like waves rolling down a waterfall. Being closer to the ground, the wee folk got the brunt of the massive attack.

The trolls and ogres started slamming their clubs on the steps, killing the squirming monsters left and right. But there were so many wigglers that Ludicra was soon leaping and flailing about like everyone else. The stings were horrible—like fire arrows piercing her pelt—and she smashed her body against the wall to kill her tormentors. That didn't bring any relief as the horrid insects continued to swarm all over her. They stung so often that Ludicra's skin began to get numb.

"They're poisonous!" she yelled over the shouts and wails. "They're trying to kill us!"

"And doing a good job!" cried Filbum, dancing around like a troll on hot coals. "What will we do?"

To her horror, Ludicra saw several gnomes drop to the steps, twitching from the terrible toxins. More and more gnomes were starting to fall, and everyone was weakening from the relentless attack. Even as they killed hundreds of the wigglers, others came streaming down the steps.

"Filbum!" she demanded. "Can you really fly?"

The young troll stared dumbly at her as he swatted wigglers on his back and chest. "Well, I . . . I think I can."

"We've seen so many traps, there's got to be another nearby," said Ludicra. "Head down the stairs, find it, and trip it. Save yourself by flying."

Filbum gulped. "But I—"

"Move it!" shouted Ludicra. "We'll be right behind you." The itchy leader grabbed Filbum and shoved him down the steps. She yelled after him, "If Weevil is all right, get her to help you!"

The troll started swatting the wigglers off Captain Chomp, knowing she would need the big ogre. "Get ahold of yourself!" ordered Ludicra. "Everyone! Grab two gnomes and run deeper! If you see a trap on the steps, jump over it!"

Ludicra didn't need to tell them twice, as everyone in the party was soon in motion, bounding down the stairs. The gnomes got a second wave of energy, and only a few of them had to be carried. Fleeing deeper into the earth in time of danger was natural to them.

Ludicra had no idea how long they tumbled pell-mell down the stairs, madly itching and smashing millipedes. But she was very relieved when she saw a lantern waving in the distant shadows.

"Watch out!" shouted Weevil's voice. "A jump is coming up!"

All of them ran faster, with waves of insects still in pursuit. Although she carried a squirming gnome covered with millipedes, Ludicra made a strong dash to safety. She saw a patch of darkness where several steps were missing and hurled herself over it.

Weevil and Filbum caught her on the other side, and kept her from sailing down a long flight of stairs. Ludicra pressed her bulk against the wall, trying to get out of the way of the panicked gnomes and pursuing insects.

The sea of millipedes was right behind them, and hundreds of them plummeted headlong into the pit. Like a hive mind, the river of bugs parted and began to run along the walls, where they were met by smashing clubs. A great squishing continued until the last gnome was across, then

Weevil grabbed her lantern. The ogre splashed a torrent of burning oil on the walls, and the delightful smell of barbecued wigglers soon filled the passageway.

Although they had outrun the horde, they were still covered with millipedes. With tooth and claw, they dealt with the enemy. While the ogres kept the swarm at bay on the other side of the pit, the trolls cooked the wigglers as fast as they could catch them. Most were burnt until they were black and crunchy, with their little singed legs sticking out.

As greasy smoke filled the stairwell, the weary travelers enjoyed another marvelous feast.

"We have to take this burrow over," Crawfleece whispered to Ludicra. She chomped down her fifteenth wiggler and spit food as she spoke. "This is the best place to live in all of Bonespittle! It even has a view of the Bonny Woods, if you like that sort of thing."

Ludicra glanced around at the stairs, which were covered with charred millipede crumbs, spiderwebs, and the slime of ages. She smiled wistfully. "Yes, it *is* a place out of some wonderful nightmare, but it belongs to everyone in Bonespittle, not just us. At least, I think that's what Rollo would say."

Crawfleece scowled, showing her fangs. "Are you still trying to convince me that you know what Rollo wants? Just because he used to drool over you and follow you around like a hungry leech? You never gave him the time of night, and now you think we should listen to *you* instead of him. Did he really ask you to marry him?"

Ludicra clanged her fangs together, trying to keep her temper. Then she noticed that all conversation and eating among her band had stopped, and the ogres and gnomes were gazing at the two of them.

The plump troll shook her head and replied, "I'm not going to fight you, Crawfleece; I'm saving my fight for the elves and fairies. When we find Rollo, you can ask him what he wants. Maybe we'll both be surprised. I just know that I want to be Rollo's queen, so I'm going to find him. If I have to think like him to do it, I will."

"Rollo thinks weird," added Weevil, with a shake of her head. "That's what we need, because the old ways of Bonespittle are dead."

"As dead as Stygius Rex," said Filbum, rising to his feet. "So let's not argue about it. Who wants mushrooms for dessert?"

"You saw mushrooms?" asked Crawfleece, perking up.

Filbum nodded. "When I was flying, I thought I saw a clump of them farther down the stairs. I'll be right back."

Chomp snorted in disbelief. "Weevil, was he really flying?"

The lanky ogre shook her head. "I was watching my feet, grabbing wigglers, and tapping the pole. I didn't see him until he sprang the trap."

"Fie on you!" scoffed Filbum. "I would have to sprout wings for you to think I was flying. I'll *walk* down and get us some mushrooms." With a sigh, the small troll grabbed a lantern and meandered down the stairs into the darkness.

"Look out for danger!" warned Ludicra.

Filbum waved back at them and slouched his shoulders. He seemed troubled at their refusal to believe he could fly, the way Rollo flew. Ludicra frowned in worry, because it was plain that Rollo's shadow hung over all of them. The longer he stayed missing, the more they all tried to be like him and take his place. What they needed was the real thing.

Still muttering to himself, Filbum wandered down the dark stairs. He was looking for mushrooms, as he'd said, but he really just wanted to get away from the rest of the band. He hadn't actually seen any mushrooms, and he wasn't sure he had flown either. But he would let them believe what they wanted to, because he knew he *could* fly. *Just maybe not very far.*

He couldn't go up with the millipedes massing beyond the trapdoor, so going down was his only choice. It was damper on this stretch of the stairs, so the young troll had hopes for mushroom dessert. *At any rate, I've got a full stomach, and I'm on a grand adventure,* he thought. *So what if they don't know how valuable I am! I'll show them what I can do.*

Suddenly Filbum heard skittering noises, and an odd draft twisted the flame in his lantern. He looked around but could see nothing except grimy stone steps and glittering ooze. There were a variety of pungent smells, but none of them were unexpected. If his stomach wasn't so full, he might have caught the rat or lizard that had made those noises. Instead Filbum decided to poke through the seepage in the corners and crevices, looking for fungi. He wanted fat, juicy mushrooms, but he could accept skinny ones.

With his club, he poked through some greenish-blue moss and sickly yellow slime. *Not enough light down here to make tasty slime,* he decided with a wrinkle of his snout. Filbum shuffled down the steps, sniffing along the stream of greenery oozing out of the corners of the stairs. So far there were no mushrooms, but he did stumble across a very interesting old boot.

Filbum gradually looked up from the boot, and found it was attached to a leg encased in bright green britches. With a gulp, his eyes drifted upward to a wide cloth belt, topped by a red shirt and green waistcoat. In between was a long bow, with an arrow cocked. The apparition was topped off by a blue-eyed, bearded face that looked unlike anyone in Bonespittle. The being was about five feet tall, a good foot smaller than Filbum, who was short for his race.

The troll leaned back and tried to smile at the stranger, who had to be an elf. Filbum's jittery grin turned into an anguished cry the moment he saw that the stairs below him were filled with armed elves. They were equally surprised, as they realized for the first time that this creature crawling in the muck was a troll.

"Help! Elves! Elven attack!" he screamed, certain he would be turned into a dung heap any moment.

Filbum scrambled up the stairs as hands grasped at his legs. He broke free just as an arrow sliced through the air. The troll ducked under two more missiles, but the fourth caught him squarely in the back. Filbum howled in anger and indignation, and though he swiped at the arrow, he couldn't reach it. In truth, the pain wasn't terrible, and it made him run all the faster.

"Elves! Fairies!" he wailed. "They're attacking!"

Ludicra and Crawfleece were the first to catch him and see the arrow sticking from his back. When the ogres caught up to them, there was already battle lust in their yellow eyes. Chomp, Weevil, and Motley brought out their shields not a moment too soon, as the dank passageway filled with whistling arrows. Most of them banged off the walls and went rattling around the band's feet.

Filbum and Ludicra found themselves crouching behind the ogres and Crawfleece, who drew their clubs and maces. Ludicra looked back to see the clever but cowardly gnomes setting grappling hooks and dropping ropes into the pit where the millipedes had fallen. In five seconds, they had disappeared.

"When the arrows stop, we charge!" bellowed Chomp. "On my command!"

Ludicra gulped, thinking that she was happy to let Chomp

take the lead. She looked at Filbum and tried to figure out how to extract the arrow from his back. He didn't seem too bothered by it—in fact, he seemed a bit giddy as, with a goofy smile, he shivered and hugged his hairy shoulders.

"Is it snowing in here?" he asked. "It's awfully cold."

"Cold?" replied Ludicra. She was sweating from fear and the closeness of the lit lanterns she was guarding. "Do you feel all right?"

"Never felt better!" He hiccuped. "I think I'll take a little nap." And with that, Filbum keeled over and was fast asleep.

Suddenly Ludicra began to worry. "Chomp!" she called over the din of the battle. "Are their arrows poisoned?"

"That's what we've always heard!" yelled the big ogre. The arrows began to ease a little, and she could see the captain heft his club and prepare for attack. "Get ready now—"

The ogres and Crawfleece tensed. There wasn't enough room in the stairway for more than the four of them to charge, so Ludicra didn't feel bad about staying with Filbum. As he lay on the steps, his shivering grew worse, and she felt certain that he'd been poisoned.

She shook him and tried to wake him up. "Filbum! Can you hear me?"

Below her, Chomp jumped to his feet and roared, "Bash their bonny little heads!"

"Elves, go home!" screeched Crawfleece.

With a blood-chilling howl, the warriors rose up and

rushed down the stairs. Ludicra was torn about what to do. She didn't want to leave Filbum, but she knew that if they didn't defeat these invaders, they would all be stuck with poison arrows.

"I'll come back," she assured Filbum, who was too busy shivering to notice. The plump troll jumped to her feet, raised her club, and waddled into battle.

CHAPTER 8
GOING DEEPER

To Ludicra, the battle was nothing but a mad blur. The ogres had the high ground and the big clubs, and the first row of elves quickly regretted their attack. Chomp, Weevil, Motley, and Crawfleece smashed them into submission, beginning a stampede in the other direction. The elves leapfrogged each other down the stairs, but they managed to regroup long enough to unleash another slew of arrows. That slowed Captain Chomp and his team, who hid behind their shields.

"Ludicra!" yelled Chomp. "Kill any we left alive!"

The young troll gulped and looked at the carnage that decorated the stairs. Four elves had splattered brains, and a fifth was wheezing from a bash to the stomach. All the air in his lungs was gone. Ludicra lifted her club to finish him off, which would have been easy, had he not gazed at her with the bluest eyes she had ever seen. Even though she had never seen blue eyes before, Ludicra knew these were the bluest in the world.

The elf's blond hair was splattered with blood, but his brains were still intact. His lithe body was bent in two, and he could barely straighten himself. "Please," he rasped. "Spare me."

Ludicra heard stomping on the stairs, and she looked up to see Captain Chomp hovering over them. He lifted his stained club and bared his tusks. "I told you to *kill* him!"

His weapon started down, and she jumped in front of the wounded elf and caught Chomp's arm. "No!" she ordered. Ludicra could see the blood lust raging in the ogre's eyes, and he barely managed to halt his attack.

His black mane bristling, Chomp stared at her. "You know nothing about war, young troll! Why spare him?"

"Because Filbum is lying up there with a poison arrow in his back." She looked at the prisoner. "It is poisoned, isn't it?"

The elf nodded grimly, and Chomp relaxed his stance. "Maybe I was hasty. So you want to trade his life for Filbum's?"

"That's the idea."

"You'd better hurry," said the prisoner, regaining his breath. "We have an antidote we can give him."

She glared at him. "How much time does he have?"

"If he were an elf, he'd be dead already," answered the fey creature. "My name is Dwayne. Let me go down to my fellows, and I'll bring back the cure."

Chomp snorted in rage. "We can't just let him go! Does he think us fools?"

Dwayne looked around at the fallen elves. "So far, we have come out the worse in this. None of you can walk down there without getting a dozen arrows in you. Let me go, and we'll save a life."

"Go!" ordered Ludicra. "But if you fail to come back, I'll chase you to the Bonny Woods myself."

The elf smiled dashingly at the rotund troll. "I believe you would." He doffed his hat and slipped past Captain Chomp, who scowled darkly at him.

"*Dwayne,* " muttered the ogre with a snort. "All of you below! Let the elf pass, and allow him to return. Alone!"

There were puzzled shouts from the darkness, but Dwayne was already skipping past them. They heard the weird twitter of birdcalls, and Ludicra realized that it was the elf, signaling his comrades.

Captain Chomp growled. "You know, we could have questioned him . . . found out why they're here."

"We'll ask him when he comes back," said Ludicra.

"Ha! When he comes back!" Chomp snorted in derisive laughter, then he grew glum. "There were a lot of elves. I fear this has become a more treacherous journey than we planned. You know, if we went back to Fungus Meadows, we could rally a huge army with our tale of elves invading Bonespittle. We could come down here in force."

Now it was Ludicra's turn to scowl. "Afraid of a few elves, are you, Captain? They know they're on our side of the Great Chasm, in the wrong place, and they have to leave."

"They had better!" blustered Chomp. "But we should warn everyone in Bonespittle."

"We'll stay on our mission," answered Ludicra sternly. "We can deal with them by ourselves." The rotund troll looked wistfully down the dank stairwell. "Besides, they may know something about Rollo."

"Ah, yes, Rollo." Chomp grunted and wiped the tip of his club on a dead elf.

Ludicra climbed the steps to check on Filbum, and was alarmed by how cold he felt. His teeth were chattering, and his lips were bluer than usual. She wrapped her brawny arms and big torso around Filbum to give him warmth. Soon his teeth stopped chattering, and he smiled; but Ludicra could feel his ragged breathing and fading heartbeat.

She heard shouts from below, and she knew it had to be Dwayne returning. "Tell him to hurry!" she shouted.

Chomp roared something, and the blond elf bounded up the stairs to Ludicra and her patient. His skin paled when he saw the shivering troll, but he set right to work pulling out the arrow. Then he unwrapped a poultice, which he applied directly to the wound. Captain Chomp watched him with suspicion and curiosity.

"Hold his mouth open," ordered the elf.

Ludicra and Chomp did as they were told, and Dwayne poured a skinful of dark, foul-smelling brew through Filbum's icy lips. Ludicra tickled the troll's throat to make him laugh and swallow. When they had forced as much medicine down him as they could, the elf, the troll, and the ogre slumped against the wall, panting wearily. Filbum fell into another sleep, but this one was without racking chills.

Ludicra noticed Gnat and another gnome poking their heads out of the pit behind her, and she motioned to the gnomes to disappear. There was no sense letting this enemy know about them. *Let that be our secret for now,* she thought.

"Will he live?" asked Ludicra.

Dwayne shook his fair head. "I don't know much about trolls, but he seems hardy. If the arrow itself didn't do much damage, he should live." The elf smiled reassuringly.

"We heal quickly," answered Ludicra. *What a stupid thing to say!* She was getting tongue-tied around the handsome stranger.

Chomp lowered his massive brow to glare at the elf. "And what are ye doing in our tunnels? This is Bonespittle, in case ye got lost."

"Yes, we know," answered the slender elf, glancing at Ludicra for protection. "I can only tell you that we're looking for something. If you make us depart, we will, because I don't think we can get past you."

"You can start departing right now!" snapped Chomp.

"Not yet," said Ludicra, gazing into Dwayne's crystal-blue eyes—as scary as the sky in bright daylight. "We're looking for something too. A troll managed to fly across the Great Chasm—his name is Rollo. Have you heard of him?".

Dwayne looked quizzically at her. "A flying troll? I believe I would have remembered that. But you should know that it has taken us many months to get this far. We haven't heard any news from home in a long time. There was an ugly fellow who fell down the chasm one day, but the fall didn't kill him. We followed him, and he led us to this passageway. He went fast, we were exploring . . . so we lost him in the tunnel."

Chomp nodded sagely. "So that is how General Drool got back to Bonespittle so fast—he took these stairs. Anything else you know about, Dwayne?"

The elf shook his head and smiled charmingly at Ludicra. "I only know that we didn't mean to attack your friend. We were startled and afraid. We aren't used to being underground, and you lose all track of time down here. We got a bit jumpy. We've had to fight dangerous creatures every step of the way."

Chomp snorted. "Are you crazy? This is like a walk in Fungus Meadows. Don't worry, you won't have to meet any more dangerous creatures, because you're leaving right now. Get your band and crawl back to your Bonny Woods."

Dwayne bowed gracefully, then stole another glance at

Ludicra. Before he could rush off, the troll grabbed the medicine skin from his hands. "Leave us this, please," said Ludicra.

He nodded and took his delicate hands off the skin. Then, without another thought, Dwayne hurried down the steps. "Let him pass!" shouted Captain Chomp.

Both of them checked on Filbum, and the young troll was sleeping peacefully. Captain Chomp walked to the pit and shouted down, "Gnat! Come up now! We have enemy bodies to throw in there."

The ogre pointed down the stairs at Weevil, Crawfleece, and Motley, who were setting up a blockade on the steps. "I don't want to take anyone off the front line for this work."

"You don't trust the elves?" asked Ludicra.

"Do you?" said Chomp. "I still say we should warn the rest of Bonespittle."

Ludicra shook her head. "There's not enough time. I just hope this doesn't slow us down."

"Right," said the ogre with a sniff. "When they come at us with five hundred archers, I'll remind you of this decision."

Ludicra said nothing more, because there wasn't much left to say. The elves had poison arrows, and they weren't afraid to use them. Not only that, but they had paid a visit to Bonespittle. Now she supposed they were even for the trip to the Bonny Woods made by Stygius Rex, General Drool, and Rollo so long ago.

The troll heard some strange trilling sounds coming from the darkness beneath them. It seemed distant, but the twisting stairwell echoed with mournful wails and high-pitched twitters. Ludicra knew instantly that it was a death song for the elves who had already departed. Her entire party grew quiet as they listened to the grating cries of grief lifting from the depths.

"Hello, Prince Thatch!" called Rollo. The troll peered glumly through the slats of an elven hut, trying to catch the leader's eye. The hut was covered with large nets and sur-rounded by archers; Rollo was still a prisoner in the Bonny Woods. "What's going to happen to me?"

The red-bearded elf considered him coldly. "That depends on what has happened to your friend, Clipper. So far there's been no sign of her, and everyone in the Bonny Woods is looking. Once we know she'll do no harm, per-haps you'll be allowed to leave."

"Maybe she's gone to Bonespittle," said Rollo.

Thatch grimaced with disgust. "Why would she do that?"

"I don't know," admitted the troll with a frustrated shrug. "But if you'll let me go, I'll find out."

The red-haired elf laughed snidely. "You'd like that, wouldn't you? I suppose you're ready to join Clipper, if she's up to no good. Why did you bring her back here and make such a fuss—to get our hopes up? You wanted us to trust you, but why?"

"I didn't think you would ever trust me," said the big troll, hanging his head. "I just wanted to bring Clipper home."

Thatch scowled. "So you could turn her evil with your cursed knife. But I admit, troll, you had us believing you for a while. Maybe you did it for the food."

"We have food back in Bonespittle," answered Rollo. "Maybe it's not as good as yours, but I didn't come all this way just to eat."

"That's what I'm afraid of," answered Prince Thatch, backing away from the prisoner. "I don't know *why* you came here, but I know you're not leaving until I find out." He waved to his elves. "Double the number of nets and the number of archers. If anyone lets the troll escape, you'll take the prisoner's place."

"Yes, sir!" shouted the elven warriors with grim determination.

"If he demands food, feed him worms and grubs," ordered the prince. "No more of our precious food."

Again the guards shouted their approval, and Rollo sunk to his haunches inside the fortified hut. He had come here only to do some good—to build bridges between Bonespittle and the Bonny Woods. Instead he had unleashed an unknown force upon both lands.

"Clipper," he whispered to the darkness, "come home. Come back to your true self. Don't let the black knife lead you." Rollo lowered his shaggy head, wondering if his plea would do any good at all.

* * *

Clipper sat on a tree stump, laughing uproariously at the sight of Stygius Rex juggling three fireballs in his hands. A thousand ogres and gnomes, and a handful of trolls, lay prostrate before him, cowering and shivering in fear as the sorcerer razed their village and burned their hovels. Flames licked the night sky, and the delightful smell of singed fur wafted on the wind. Just for fun, the demented fairy threw a spell and made a bunch of gnomes start sneezing.

"So what will it be?" asked Stygius Rex, tossing a fireball into their berry patch. The scraggly thicket blew up in a spangle of searing embers, and the cold air suddenly roared with heat. "Will you follow this stupid troll who has run off—*again!*—or will you follow me, your old master?"

"You! You!" they shouted, scraping and bowing in the mud. "Hail, Stygius Rex! Long live Stygius Rex!"

"That's better." With a sneer, the sorcerer flipped his last two fireballs over his back, and they blew up the privy, spewing muck everywhere. A stench wafted over Bonespittle, announcing that terror had returned to the land.

"Sergeant Skull!" intoned the sorcerer. He pointed to a grizzled ogre who had a metal bowl covering his skull. Shuddering, the old warrior crawled forward, and the sorcerer asked, "Do we still have enemies? Will anyone stand against us?"

The veteran nodded his shiny head, touching the ground with his snout. "One band stands against us," he rasped. "Chomp and Weevil, plus some gnomes and trolls.

They went off to find Rollo and rescue him."

"Yes, he probably needs rescuing by now!" chirped Clipper. The ogres and gnomes stared at the fairy, trembling even more in the presence of the revived fairy.

Stygius Rex stroked his warty chin. "So that pretender still has followers? I suppose I will have to deal with them before I tighten my grip on the land. Sergeant Skull, you and your warriors spread the word: Stygius Rex is back! Bonespittle is ignoble once again!"

"Aye, master!" shouted the old ogre, bowing before the sorcerer.

"And get those trolls back to work!" ordered Stygius Rex as he surveyed the smoldering wreckage he had caused. "This place is falling apart." With that, the sorcerer winked at Clipper, and the fairy squeaked with mirth.

It's amazing, she thought, *that an old sorcerer and a revived fairy could take over a whole world with a few fireballs and sneezing spells. What cowards they are! It's true— being a bad fairy is a lot more fun than being a good fairy.*

"Something glittering lies ahead," whispered Gnat. The young gnome and two more wee folk had taken the lead in the party's descent. Ludicra and Chomp were right behind the scouts, who were tapping poles upon the steps to test for traps. By now, they had gotten very good at detecting and jumping over the hidden pits, and most of the traps remained unsprung.

Ludicra peered into the steamy gloom of the dank stairwell. The stone walls felt hot here, and steam spurted from cracks in the rock, as if a river of molten lava surged on the other side. The heat in the tunnel was like the breath of some behemoth living in the bowels of the planet. Ludicra could see that the passageway leveled into a dark chamber, the kind they had come to dread.

Still the ogres pushed forward, anxious to plunge everyone into some new battle or adventure. Ludicra followed behind Captain Chomp, with Gnat at her side. Farther back, among the gnomes, Crawfleece helped Filbum walk down the stairs. Crawfleece's attitude toward the dumpy troll had changed completely since his encounter with the elves and near death. Ludicra was certain that Filbum was more fit than he pretended and was simply enjoying the attention of the brawny female. Ludicra let it slide.

The old Ludicra would have chided Filbum, made him admit he was malingering. But this new Ludicra had grown up a lot in the last few weeks. Appearances, status, safety— they were as wispy as the hot fog all around her. Life could be turned over in an instant, and all that counted was being a loyal friend. This haggard band of trolls, ogres, and gnomes were more real to her than any day of her past fifteen years. Her whole life before now seemed like a vague dream . . . of wasted time and petty concerns.

"By the Great Chasm! Look at that!" shouted Chomp. The ogres rushed toward a sparkling pool of light in the corner of the soggy cavern. As she drew closer, Ludicra could see a pile of glittering gold and sparkling jewels, lit with an aura of wonder. The ogres charged toward it, and Ludicra almost started to as well, but little Gnat punched her in the thigh.

"Tell them to stop!" he ordered nervously. Crawfleece and Filbum arrived at that moment, gaping in awe at the wondrous find. "It's dangerous!" cried Gnat.

Ludicra blinked off the spell of the treasure and turned to shout, "Chomp . . . Weevil . . . Motley! Stay back!"

But her words had no effect as the three ogres raced toward the glittering hoard, shoving each other and laughing. All of them stumbled at once and went crashing into the gleaming pile, which exploded like one of the sorcerer's fireballs. Globs of flame came sailing toward Ludicra and her comrades, and all they could do was duck.

CHAPTER 9

FROM THE FRYING PAN INTO THE FIRE

S HRIEKING IN PAIN, THEIR PELTS AFLAME, THE THREE OGRES came roaring out of the cavern. Ludicra thought they would stampede over her, but the gnomes made themselves useful by tripping the ogres. Chomp, Weevil, and Motley sprawled upon the floor, allowing the others to cover them with dust, drinking water, and their own bodies.

Ludicra personally fell upon Captain Chomp and tried to reassure him as she smothered the burning oil in his fur. "You're all right. You're alive!" she assured him. "Get control of yourself, Captain."

"It was a booby trap!" panted Gnat. "Maybe an *enchanted* booby trap. You couldn't help yourselves." The gnome glanced at Ludicra and winked, so that she knew he was making it up. At least it gave the ogres a chance to excuse their stupidity.

"Those wicked elves!" grumbled Chomp. "This is their doing . . . intended to slow us down."

"No doubt," answered Ludicra as she rolled off the singed ogre. "If not the elves, who else could have done it?"

"And why a treasure?" asked Filbum. "Do they think we're looking for treasure?"

"No, but maybe *they* are!" crowed Crawfleece. She patted Filbum affectionately on the head. "Oh, you're so smart."

He blushed a deep shade of purple, while Ludicra studied the wounded ogres. "Get some eel grease on those burns," she suggested. "Captain Chomp, can you tell me why you all fell down at once?"

"We tripped," answered the ogre. He looked at his fellows for confirmation, and they nodded.

"I bet it was a trip wire," added Weevil. "It must have lit a fuse." She shook the smoldering embers off her pelt and staggered to her feet. "You know, a bunch of elf heads would look good in my den."

"The best way to foil their plans is to keep moving," declared Ludicra. "They are searching for *something,* and we're spoiling it for them. Let's find the stairs."

Wearily the party picked themselves up from the cavern floor, which was littered with fake baubles and burnt bits of rag. Seen after the fact, the trap was more amusing than deadly, and many of the gnomes congratulated each other on their bravery. After a few moments, the ogres laughed too, and Chomp and Weevil blamed each other for leading the greedy charge.

After searching in the smoke and sulfurous mist for several minutes, the gnomes found the stairs down. Once again, they descended into the moldy darkness, and Ludicra hoped they were getting close to the bottom.

The Enchantress Mother frowned sadly at Rollo, then lowered her head. "I'm sorry," she whispered hoarsely. "There's nothing I can do. The council is meeting to pass judgment on you."

"But what kind of judgment?" asked Rollo from inside his prison. The hut was covered with so many nets and mats that he could barely see the white-haired elf in her flowing pale gown.

Melinda grimaced. "I only know that many would like your death—not just for this visit but for the last one too. They trace many of our woes to your first coming, and now we don't know what has become of Clipper . . . or the black knife. Many say you've brought a curse to our land. Please understand, they are afraid."

"So am I!" exclaimed Rollo. "I don't think you can solve your problems by punishing me. Can't you reason with them? They respect you."

"Not anymore," said the Enchantress Mother sadly. "Not since I aided you in resurrecting Clipper. When you practice magic, you are always suspect if that magic goes awry. They respect me, but fear me too."

Suddenly there came a burst of voices, and a loud discussion flowed from the lodge hut into the village pathways. Rollo could barely make out Prince Thatch in the mob of elves, who were peppering him with questions. It looked more like chaos than a meeting, but Rollo tried to be hopeful.

"I must go," whispered the Enchantress Mother. "Be brave, Rollo." She waved and melted into the crowd as the imperious prince strode up to Rollo's prison.

The bearded elf glared righteously at him. "The Council of the Red Garter Button and Green Sash Pin have met to discuss your punishment."

"My punishment?" asked Rollo. "What crime have I done?"

"I'm coming to that!" snapped Prince Thatch. "You are accused of trespassing in the Bonny Woods, inciting a war, starting careless fires, and resurrecting a dead fairy without permission."

"You were there!" exclaimed Rollo. "We had *your* permission."

"You didn't have the permission of the Council of the Red Garter Button and Green Sash Pin!" intoned Thatch, talking more to the crowd than Rollo. "It takes time to assemble them, and now they have spoken. We all agree— it's illegal to resurrect dead fairies with cursed knives."

The prince straightened his green waistcoat and glared anew at Rollo. "Five days from now, with the rise of the Kissing Moon, nineteen of our best archers will use you for target practice. Since you're such a big target, we'll adjust the range. I trust your death will be swift, and that it will end this curse."

"There's no curse," muttered Rollo, slumping onto his haunches. "Killing me won't make your lives better. Bad things can still happen, even in the Bonny Woods."

The regal elf spread his fingers. "Five days, troll, until the moon is right. You will be fed better, but no more visitors. Make peace, or whatever you trolls do."

"Fine," muttered Rollo, picking the straw out of his toe talons. And then he began to plan his escape.

"Be careful!" shouted Ludicra, and this time everyone stopped at her warning, especially the ogres. They stared at a fat treasure chest leaning across two steps. A stout wooden chest with thick metal bands and a shiny clasp, it looked new and completely alien in these dingy surroundings.

"Why has this turned into a treasure hunt?" asked Weevil. "Gnat, what should we do with it?"

"I would advise shoving it down the stairs," answered the gnome. "If anything happens, it will be farther down the steps."

"What if there's real treasure in it?" asked Filbum. "I mean, anything is possible in this paradise."

"Then we'll pick it up off the stairs," answered Chomp. "Someone give me a long pole."

Gnat handed him the longest they had, and the big ogre jammed it into the wooden chest and pushed. It was so heavy that he couldn't budge it, and he needed Weevil's help to finally edge it off the steps. The big box went careening down the stairs, throwing off sparks and finally smashing open far below them. At once, a noxious green cloud floated upward to engulf the party, making them cough and gag.

"Mmmmm," said Crawfleece with appreciation. "They stunk up the hall for us. That was nice of them, for once."

"It's making me homesick for the swamp," replied Filbum, taking a deep breath of the greenish fog.

"And more fake treasure," said Weevil with a scowl. "What's the point of this?"

"It would seem they want to discourage us from looking for treasure," answered Ludicra. "I say we catch those cowardly elves!" *Maybe I'll see Dwayne again,* she thought.

With a rousing chorus of battle cries, the ogres, trolls, and gnomes charged down the stairs into the smelly unknown.

The heat and steam in the tunnel grew steadily worse, until it was like walking through the Dismal Swamp in the summer. Still, the tunnel party kept up a fast pace, hoping to catch the elves and pay them back for the tricks they'd been pulling. The stairs finally gave way to a sloping passage similar to the one at the top. Now they made even better time, because they didn't have to search for booby traps.

"Hold up!" cautioned Chomp, pointing down the tunnel at a blinding white light. "What is *that?*"

Ludicra, Crawfleece, and everyone else stopped and stared in wonder. Although the light was diffused by a smoky mist, none of them had ever seen anything so bright.

"Yuck . . . daylight," said Gnat with disappointment. "Does this mean our dungeon romp is finished?"

"Awwww," groaned everyone sadly.

Filbum sniffed. "I don't want to leave. It's so agreeable here!"

"All bad things must come to an end," said Ludicra. "There can only be sunlight down this far when the sun is right overhead. Come on . . . but be careful going out the hole into daylight. There might be an ambush."

"I suggest ogres with shields raised," said Chomp, stepping ahead of the others.

"After you, Captain." Ludicra swept her claw downward.

Weevil and Motley joined Chomp, and the three ogres advanced toward the ominous white light. Having not seen daylight in many days—how many they had no idea—the band had to shield their eyes as they approached the exit. Chomp muscled his way past the other two ogres and stepped bravely into the sunlight. They heard a dozen *thunks*, and he ducked back inside.

Chomp showed them his shield, which had a dozen arrows sticking from it. "I think they're still out there."

Shielding her eyes from the horrible light, Ludicra edged closer to the opening to get a better look at the bottom of the Great Chasm. A bubbling, oozing river of lava flowed down the center of the canyon—it was hard to tell how wide it was. Twisted, misshapen plants decorated sulfurous springs and cauldronlike pools of boiling water. The landscape was dotted with huge black boulders, and a wretched yellow fog hung over everything. It was also hot . . . very hot.

Ludicra ducked back inside. "It looks all right," she said. "I couldn't see anybody."

"Like you said, the sun must be directly overhead," said Weevil with disgust. "In a few minutes, this whole canyon will be back in shadow."

Ludicra took another quick look, risking only her shaggy head. She saw a lithe figure scramble over one of the black rocks and jump off the other side. Ludicra stuck her head farther out and saw more figures dashing into the yellow mist.

"They're running away!" she yelled. "We have to catch them. Ogres first."

Chomp, Weevil, and Motley charged out of the cave entrance, their shields in front of them. No arrows struck them, so the three trolls followed, with eight gnomes bringing up the rear. Now a couple of arrows sailed toward them, landing short, and Ludicra knew they were shooting on the run. Weevil grabbed her bow from her back and sent a couple of arrows after the fleeing elves.

"Help! Argh!" screamed a gnome behind Ludicra.

The troll whirled around to see that one of their party had been caught by the leaves and vines of a monstrous plant. As gnomes surrounded their comrade, spiked leaves closed upon his body, and the vines squeezed him like a nest of pythons. Shrieking, the gnomes attacked the monstrous plant with knives and claws, and a royal battle ensued.

Ludicra looked helplessly at the trolls and ogres, still pursuing the elves into the sickly fog. The heat made her pelt all prickly. "Gnat, get him free and stay here!" she ordered. "We'll be right back!"

Gnat was too busy biting one of the vines to reply. The predatory plant now had two more gnomes in its clutches, but it wasn't given much time to enjoy its meal. The gnomes attacked it with surprising ferocity, like feral chickens.

With reluctance, Ludicra ran off after the larger members of her party. She hated to split up her band, but they had to catch the elves or risk ambushes and traps every step of the way. Through the rotten-egg stench they ran, pursuing lithe figures who were barely visible in the swirling yellow fog. The lava river burped and belched beside them, adding scalding steam and burnt ash to the thick air.

The infernal canyon and mad chase were like a dream, thought Ludicra, especially in the eerie daylight. She looked up and couldn't even see the rim of the chasm, but a broad shadow was slipping down the steep rock face. As Weevil had predicted, the sun's trip over the gorge was intense but brief. Suddenly a monstrous shadow engulfed them, and the jagged landscape was plunged into twilight.

Only this was a twilight that lasted for hours as it gradually mutated into darkness. It seemed as if they ran for hours, tripping and stumbling along the rocky path, fighting plants that kept trying to eat them. Ludicra saw an elf's hat and bow resting at the base of one contented-looking weed.

"They're crossing the river!" shouted Weevil somewhere ahead of them. "They have a bridge!"

That made the trolls' footsteps quicken, because they were anxious to see what kind of bridge the elves would build—especially over a river of fire. Ludicra caught up with the ogres, Crawfleece, and Filbum at the burning bank of the lava river. In the twilight and steaming fog, they could barely see the last of the elves scamper across a crude rope-and-plant bridge.

Ludicra's heart sank, because it looked as if the flimsy bridge wouldn't hold even one troll or ogre. Plus several elves were atop a boulder on the other side, ready to cut the ropes as soon as their last comrade got across. The stream of molten rock was a good fifty feet across, and falling in would be certain death. Weevil shot a few arrows at the fleeing elves, but the missiles vanished into the fading light.

Finally the elves cut the ropes, and the bridge collapsed into the river, where it flamed like a fireball. Fire ran up the ropes to the boulder where the bridge was tied near

Ludicra, and the wooden planks blazed before it sank.

From the other side, the elves waved and hooted. "We're on *our* side, and you're on *your* side!" they shouted. "Make sure you keep it that way!"

"Cowards!" roared Chomp. "Mealy worms!"

He was greeted by hoots and laughter, and the dim figures retreated into the shadows. One elf whose hair gleamed brighter than that of the others lingered behind, and he doffed his green hat. "It was a pleasure to meet you, Lady Ludicra!" With that, he scampered after his fellows, and the troll blushed. Then she stomped angrily.

"Isn't there any other way across?" demanded Ludicra.

Crawfleece snorted. "There's an erupting volcano to the south and an impassable ice glacier to the north. Plus more volcanos in between."

"*They* built a bridge!" exclaimed Chomp. "Why can't we?"

"Oh, we can," answered Crawfleece. "Only it will take days to find materials, if there are any down here. Then it will take more days to build. We'll have to be really careful—we need experienced trolls, like Krunkle."

Chomp gaped at them. "None of you can build a bridge? What good are you?"

"Stifle it," said Weevil. "It's not their fault. How did we expect to get across this, anyway?"

"It's *my* fault," answered Ludicra glumly. "We should have brought a finished bridge with us."

"There wasn't exactly a lot of time for that," said

Filbum. "Look, we've achieved the first part of our mission—we're at the bottom of the chasm. Not only that, but we chased the invaders back to their side. Let's celebrate our victory!"

"Yes," agreed Chomp, brightening a bit. "Let's rest . . . and eat. We need to do some scouting, too."

"We need to see if we have any gnomes left," said Ludicra worriedly.

By the time the ogres and trolls tromped back to the entrance of the tunnel, it was pitch-dark at the bottom of the canyon. The only light was the fiery crust that floated on the river of lava, but it was enough for them. As they drew closer, they saw a fire burning in the blackness high off the ground—it appeared to be on top of one of the boulders. The warriors drew their weapons and stalked silently toward the flames.

Chomp and Ludicra went first, and they found the gnomes gathered solemnly around the burning rock. Chomp lowered his weapon and said, "Funeral pyre. They must have lost a comrade, but to what enemy?"

"The plants," answered Ludicra. "We fought through them, but we're a lot bigger." She motioned the rest of the band forward, and they joined the gnomes in the solemn gathering.

Gnat looked at them and nodded. "The plants killed two, plus we never mourned the others we lost. Did you catch those devilish elves?"

"No," Ludicra answered grimly. "They had a bridge, which they burned after them."

Gnat shrugged wearily and lifted his voice in a shrill song. One by one, the other gnomes joined in, while the ogres offered low bass harmony. Like most trolls, Ludicra had never really lived among gnomes and ogres, so their customs were strange. This burning of the dead would not have taken place in the Dismal Swamp, when there were so many bog beasts who were eager to help with disposal.

This dreary song could even be for the end of our quest, thought Ludicra. *We have no way to go on from here, and we're tired and injured. I'm farther away than ever from Rollo.*

After the service, they retired to the tunnel to eat their rations of gopher jerky and get some rest. Even though it was dark outside, the springs and lava flow made the night as hot as the day. It was unbearably hot inside the passage, and the band spread some distance up the incline. Ludicra didn't even know where Crawfleece and Filbum had gone.

She curled up near the entrance, behind Chomp. They posted no guard, because it seemed clear that no one would bother them down here. The bottom of the Great Chasm was the most remote place in either land. Even so, the ogres piled their shields in front of the entrance, mostly to ward off the heat.

Ludicra fell into a fitful sleep, in which she had dreams that were altogether too pleasant. At one point, a tiny, elegant fairy came to visit her, and the specter was so vivid that it seemed real. Ludicra knew without being told that this was Rollo's friend Clipper.

"You are very brave," cooed the fairy into her floppy ear.

"Is my beloved well?" asked Ludicra groggily.

"Quite so, but not for long," answered the little voice. "We are going to help you tomorrow during daylight, when I can tell you more. For now, sleep and rest. You will be with Rollo soon."

That brought Ludicra fully awake, and she thought she saw a shadow dart between the shields into the darkness. Chomp shook himself awake and stared at her. "What is it?" asked the ogre, grabbing his club. "What did you see?"

"Did *you* see anything?" she asked sheepishly.

"Just you jumping around," he answered.

The young troll shook her head. "It was a dream . . . about a fairy. It almost seemed real."

"Are your feet itching?" asked Chomp.

"No."

"Then it wasn't real. Go back to sleep." With a grunt, the ogre rolled over and started snoring immediately.

Not real, Ludicra told herself. *Still, it would be a relief to get some help from somewhere, even a dead fairy.*

CHAPTER 10

ESCAPE!

AT NIGHT A DOZEN ARCHERS SURROUNDED THE HUT WHERE Rollo was kept prisoner, but they couldn't see him as well as they did during the day. So he could dig with both hands and feet. During the day, he dug with only his feet, while he kept his torso facing his guards. They apparently didn't know how well trolls—and everyone in Bonespittle— could dig in the ground. It was second nature to them.

After three days of burrowing, he had carved a cavity under the wall that was big enough to squeeze into. A few more hours of digging, he knew, and he could break through the ground on the other side of the hut. Of course, he would come out only a few feet beyond the wall—he'd be in plain view of at least three archers. He would have to fly to escape, and fly fast.

So Rollo also practiced flying at night when they couldn't see him. With concentration, the troll found, he was able to elevate a few feet off the ground. When he had open sky above him, he was certain, he could soar high and pick up speed as he went. His escape would also depend upon a diversion.

During the day, Rollo enjoyed the fruits and grains they gave him, but he was careful to save his seeds. He found that he could dry them in the slivers of sunlight that slipped between the slats, then toss a few of them out for the birds at night. The little birds that came to visit weren't enough to bother his guards, if they even saw them. But he was saving the majority of his seeds for the diversion he needed, because the elves were afraid of too many birds at once.

It was nearly dawn, and the troll knew he had only two more days to live, and one night. He worried that if he waited until the last minute, his guard would be doubled, or they would move him. *No,* he decided finally, *it's best to go tonight.*

There was something about the hour just before dawn that Rollo had always liked. That was *his* time . . . a time to dream and plan. It was also a time to escape. He burrowed into the crawl space under the wall of his hut and pushed up at the earth on the other side. He didn't want to attract any attention but needed to make sure that he could break through. Shaking the dirt from his hair and face, Rollo crawled back into the hut.

Now he gathered up his seeds and pushed a few of them through the slats. For three nights, he had enticed the birds to come, and now there were more than ever. With a deep breath, the determined troll flung all his seeds out of the hut onto the dirt. At once, a sizable flock of squawking birds landed and began pecking.

"Birds!" yelled Rollo in a high-pitched voice, trying to sound like an elf. The guards reacted by shouting and running, and Rollo dashed back into his hole.

Hearing the cries of the archers, Rollo figured they were distracted enough. Using all his strength, he pushed his way through the last inches of dirt, until his head and shoulders poked from the ground. As more shouts disturbed the peaceful night, Rollo concentrated upon making himself fly. He pictured himself zooming through the air, and a moment later, he was!

As he rose from the hole, the troll saw a startled elf right in front of him. The archer tried to draw an arrow, but the troll kicked the bow out of his hands. Two more archers reacted slowly and fumbled with their weapons. By the time they shot their missiles, Rollo was twenty feet in the air and zooming away. The arrows arced under his feet, as alarm bells pealed throughout the village.

I'm free! the troll told himself happily. It was dark, and he didn't know where he was going—so he concentrated on gaining altitude. *Nobody can stop me now!*

That was when his nose began to run, and he sneezed.

Then his feet grew terribly itchy, and he tried to scratch them while flying. Rollo didn't realize what all this meant until it was too late. Suddenly he was mobbed by a ferocious flock of fairies, who jabbed him with little blades and beat him on the face and ears. Now it was Rollo who was terribly distracted, and he began to drop from the sky.

The vengeful fairies plagued him until he couldn't fly anymore. His entire body was itching by the time the poor troll plummeted into the trees. "Arrrgh!" he cried as he crashed through the branches. "Achoo! Help me! Achoo!"

Even after he landed in a heap on the bottom branch, the fairies bedeviled him unmercifully. It was almost a relief when the angry elves reached him and shooed the fairies away. One of the fey folk gave him a final punch in the nose, then the elves dragged him out of the tree and threw him to the ground.

"So you thought you could get away!" said Prince Thatch triumphantly. "And you thought I had only elves watching you. Ha! You're more clever than I thought, troll, but not clever enough. Tie him up! We'll keep him in full sight from now on."

His body aching, one eye swollen, and the taste of blood in his mouth, Rollo was hauled back to the village. As he bounced along the ground, the bedraggled troll was without hope. He was all but certain that he would become the main attraction in an elven archery contest.

* * *

Ludicra gazed upward at a sheer cliff that stretched out of sight into the shadows and mist above them. She was waiting for daylight, which shined for less than an hour at the bottom of the Great Chasm. The young troll didn't know why she should care if daylight came, because that dream last night had not been real. Besides, how could a fairy help a party of ogres, trolls, and gnomes to cross a river of lava and scale an impossible cliff? That was a lot harder to do than cast a sneezing spell.

The trolls were supposed to be surveying the canyon for a bridge, while the ogres scouted for the enemy and the gnomes looked for more secret passageways. So far that day none of them had worked very hard, because it seemed hopeless. Even the absence of the elves made this stench-filled inferno seem more lonely than before.

We're fools for coming here, thought Ludicra.

Someone slapped her on the back, and she turned to see Crawfleece. "Cheer up—we'll get out of here."

"How?" asked Ludicra. "We can go back to Bonespittle . . . as failures. Even if we could get across the lava, how are we going to climb that wall?" She pointed to the other side of the Great Chasm, where a precipitous cliff awaited them.

Crawfleece smiled. "I don't know, but Rollo would find a way. And you want to be like Rollo, don't you?"

"I would settle for *finding* Rollo," answered Ludicra. "I'd like to leave the hero business to him, but I don't have any choice."

"What is that?" squeaked a gnome, drawing their attention to a group of miners on top of a black boulder. One of them pointed straight up and toward the Bonny Woods side of the canyon.

Ludicra peered upward and saw the sun sliding rapidly down the cliff face. At the same time, a huge black cloud descended with it, and the misty air was filled with loud caws and chirps. At once, the gnomes all dove for cover and the ogres came running from wherever they had been napping.

"What is that?" asked Chomp, rubbing his eyes sleepily.

"I don't know," answered Ludicra. "It looks like one of the armies that fought in the chasm that one night. Maybe they've moved the battle down here."

"Those are some big birds," said Crawfleece in amazement. Then she licked her lips. "I bet they taste just like lizard guts."

"They may have the same idea about us," added Weevil. "Get the shields, and the rest of you take cover!"

Even though they were supposed to hide, Ludicra didn't feel any danger from this approaching flock. From their sounds, it was clear that they were birds—birds of every color, shape, and size. Some were massive, with a wingspan of fifteen feet, and others were small and bright, like confetti dropping from the rim of the canyon. She glanced the other way and saw no evidence of a similar flock of fairies.

As the speckled cloud and the bright sunlight drew closer, Ludicra could see ropes and vines trailing from the mouths of the larger fliers. Smaller birds helped carry these trinkets too—it seemed as if all of them were cooperating to deliver the strands to the visitors.

"Lower your weapons!" ordered Ludicra. "I don't think they mean us any harm."

"Then what are they doing with ropes?" asked Chomp doubtfully.

It was hard not to flee as the huge flock blocked out the newly arrived sun, but the trolls and ogres held their ground. In waves, the birds landed on the boulders and scraggly plants, trying to avoid those that wanted to eat them. Ludicra realized that the bottom of the Great Chasm was not alien to these creatures—that they could come here whenever they wished.

Among the birds, Ludicra saw a white one that was startling in its beauty. Then she squinted her eyes at the apparition, because it seemed to have arms and legs. Chomp growled and lifted his club.

"That's a fairy, methinks," declared the ogre.

"Among all these birds?" asked Ludicra in wonder. When the white-gowned being swooped closer, she gasped, because it was the fairy from her dream last night.

"Clipper!" she exclaimed.

"None other," answered the fairy, alighting on an onyx boulder. She made a proper curtsy. "I am Rollo's friend—I visited you last night."

Chomp gaped at Ludicra. "You *did* see something."

"Is Rollo all right?" asked Ludicra anxiously. "Have you seen him?"

The fairy's tiny, perfect face grew troubled. "Alas, I have seen Rollo. Everybody can see him, because he's chained to a pillory in the middle of an elven village. He is well now, but he is scheduled to die tomorrow night."

"Oh, no!" gasped Ludicra, wringing her claws. "Why would they kill the Troll King?"

"It's a long story!" harped another voice. Ludicra turned to see a large green fowl preening his feathers. The talking bird went on, "The elves are stupid and cowardly, that's why! Believe me, they'll kill him all right . . . if we don't help you."

"Who are you?" demanded Crawfleece, drooling as she eyed the splendiferous creature.

"I'm Kendo," answered the bird. "I'm enchanted, was once a fairy—that's also a long story. Our main problem is with the elves, not the fairies, but they send the fairies to fight us."

"Are you working together?" asked Ludicra, pointing from Clipper to Kendo.

"Oh, yes, we're on the same side now," answered the fairy with a wink at her feathered friend. "The important thing is that we can fly, and we can carry most of you to the rim. Way up there." She pointed to the top, which was ablaze in sunlight at high noon, like a river of light.

Chomp glanced at the extreme heights and gulped.

"Well, thanks, I'm sure we've got some trolls who like to fly." He pushed Filbum forward. "Let me know how it comes out."

"No, Captain Chomp, we need you," insisted Ludicra. "How many of us can you take?"

"Hmmm," said Kendo, studying the intrepid band. "You're bigger than I thought you would be. We could probably carry seven of you aloft. It's a long flight to the top, and the wind currents are often treacherous."

"Ludicra," came a voice from behind her. The troll turned around and looked down to see Gnat. "My gnomes would prefer to stay behind, although I will go with you."

She nodded. "All right, they can stay behind and guard the tunnel. Make repairs and such."

Gnat nodded gratefully. "Thank you, mistress."

"So we have five big ones and a little one," said Kendo with a nod of his yellow beak. "That should do."

"Motley, you go," said Chomp, pushing his underling forward.

"No, no, Captain Chomp, it has to be *you*." Ludicra batted her bloodshot eyes at him. "Motley should stay and help the gnomes. Please, Captain—it will be the adventure of a lifetime."

"The *last* adventure of a lifetime," muttered the ogre. He turned to his most trusted companion. "Are you going, Weevil?"

The lanky ogre nodded. "Our journey is only half over.

As long as we've come this far, we might as well see the Bonny Woods."

The ogre's beefy shoulders slumped in resignation. "Count me in." He turned to the fairy and shook a talon at the ethereal being. "If this is a trick to kill us, I'll take you with us."

"No trick," Clipper assured him; she looked hurt by the accusation. "Didn't I help Rollo? Didn't I *die* to help you cast off Stygius Rex? What more proof do you need?"

"And how did you come back?" asked Weevil suspiciously.

"Rollo brought me back with the black knife," answered the fairy cheerfully. "Believe me, everything will work out perfectly, if you can save Rollo. The elves won't be expecting you."

Still none of the trolls and ogres looked eager to take to the sky, carried by a menagerie of feathered fowls. "Come on!" Ludicra exhorted them. "Rollo would do it for you. There are thousands of birds, and we have climbing ropes and harnesses, plus all these vines. We can make it to the top!"

One by one, the trolls and ogres nodded, along with the brave gnome Gnat. Kendo squawked, and the birds began to flap their wings in anticipation.

"Let's hurry!" urged Clipper. "We don't want to waste all this cheery daylight."

By the time the shadows began to slide down the canyon walls, six members of the band were trussed up like squid sausages. Ropes and vines hung from each and were tied to dozens of birds. Each of the strangers was attached to at least one of the giant condors, with their fifteen-foot wingspan. That made all of them feel a little better.

"Can we try a test first?" asked Chomp nervously.

Filbum started to raise his claw, but Ludicra waved him down. "I'll go first," she said. "If we ever see that crazy Rollo, you tell him what I did to be his queen." She checked the ropes, which bound her to a condor plus thirty other birds, including the talking parrot, Kendo.

"No problem," said the green bird. "You're going to fly like a kite. Wait until we catch a good draft."

Ludicra gulped. "Whatever." She glanced over at Crawfleece and said, "This is being more like Rollo than I intended."

Crawfleece laughed. "I'm right behind you!"

Growing impatient, Kendo squawked, and the great condor spread its wings. All the other birds began to flap, pulling the ropes and vines taut. Ludicra shrieked with surprise when her feet lifted off the ground, even though she'd seen it coming. Swiftly she rose, leaving her stomach behind; Ludicra was glad she hadn't eaten much. The harnesses and ropes barely cut into the troll's thick hide, and she felt no discomfort . . . until she looked down.

The raging, burning, crusty river of lava loomed directly beneath her, and Ludicra fought the urge to flail in panic. *The birds don't want to go down there either,* she told herself, *and we're still climbing.* Ludicra looked up instead, but she saw that the birds were laboring and struggling to gain altitude in the hot, misty air. *Best to look straight ahead.*

To take her mind off this scary flight, Ludicra twisted her neck around until she saw the talking bird. "Kendo!" she called. "There were elves in the Great Chasm. On our side! What were they doing down here?"

Between puffs of air and sweeps of his impressive wings, the bird shouted down, "Silly elves! They were looking for treasure, as usual. The way elves love treasure, you'd think they were part dragon."

"Treasures and dragons?" said Ludicra in wonder. "Do those things really exist?"

"Only down here!" answered Kendo. He suddenly stopped flapping madly and began to glide on open wings.

The troll looked around and saw all the birds now gliding, their wings full of air; yet they were rising faster than ever. She looked down and back, where her comrades were also rising from the burning depths. Each one was like a balloon tethered to a cloud. From here, the lava river seemed to scourge the entire canyon, and Ludicra marveled at the size of the flaming gorge. She could feel the hot air pushing against her body as they soared upward.

"Finally a decent draft!" crowed Kendo. "Now I can relax and talk to you, kiddo. You trolls don't seem to know nothin' about the Great Chasm."

"We don't," admitted Ludicra. "Please tell me."

"Long ago, there was no Great Chasm," squawked the bird. "And you folks were always beating up the elves and fairies. So they hid in the Bonny Woods and paid a huge treasure to the old Troll King to leave them alone forever."

"An old Troll King?" asked Ludicra excitedly. "He's real too?"

"That's what I said, didn't I?" snapped Kendo. "The Troll King hired an elemental sorcerer named Batmole to cause a volcanic eruption. This chasm was created on purpose, just to keep our lands apart. So Batmole did his job, and he did it well. The glacier melted, and there was a flood—and all of it carved the Great Chasm."

The bird shook his plumed head. "Now the story gets interesting. Even though all this happened as planned, the Troll King's treasure was stolen before it ever reached him. According to all our legends, the treasure was hidden somewhere in the Great Chasm, but it was never found. When the Troll King couldn't pay Batmole what he was owed, the angry sorcerers banded together and took over Bonespittle. Or so the story goes."

Ludicra gasped. Here was the real story behind the sorcerers' reign over Bonespittle, plus the rise of Stygius Rex! Eventually he got rid of all the other sorcerers and turned the trolls into slaves. He wanted everyone to forget the missing treasure, which rightfully belonged to the trolls. *We forgot and we have suffered for it!* decided Ludicra.

The very thought of treasure made her greedy heart beat

faster, but she knew she had to save Rollo first. There would be time for treasure hunts later, when she was queen.

"How much longer?" she asked.

"With these currents, we should be there in less than an hour," answered the green bird.

"Hurry!" urged Ludicra.

Kendo flapped his wings faster, but it was a long haul to the rim. At one point, Ludicra saw a huge shadow cross over them, but when she looked up it was gone. Far above her, the sky was bright blue. As they climbed through the vast canyon, the birds and their squirming cargo were little more than dots in the mist.

CHAPTER 11
FALLING IN THE FOREST

T HE FLIGHT UP THE GREAT CHASM WAS EXCITING BUT seemed to last several lifetimes. Ludicra kept looking down for her comrades, and she saw the birds struggling to carry Captain Chomp up the face of the cliff. Suddenly a rope broke on the captain's harness, and two birds whizzed past her like slingshot bullets. She feared the big ogre would plunge to the bottom, but a huge condor snapped the rope connecting him to Gnat, then flew to the ogre's aid.

The mammoth bird grabbed a rope in his mouth and took over for one of Chomp's smaller birds. By the time they got organized, his flock had dropped far beneath the others, but they never hit the lava, which writhed through the canyon like a snake on fire.

When her own birds began to struggle, Ludicra kept her

eyes on her comrades. The young troll didn't fully let out her breath until they'd risen high enough to see the trees of the Bonny Woods. The forest was a splash of vibrant green, bathed in golden sunlight, which crowned the barren cliff like a wreath. The lush greenery looked alien yet oddly pleasant, and she didn't know whether to enjoy it or be repulsed by its sweet smells and gentle breezes.

"We have to set you down!" shouted Kendo. "We don't want to be spotted."

Ludicra nodded, because reaching the ground was all right with her. The birds had picked a clearing just beyond the first row of trees. It looked as if it had once been a village, although nothing was left of the huts but outlines in the ground. Here and there were scorched stars, as if something had exploded—*perhaps a fireball,* thought Ludicra.

They had to fly over the trees to reach the clearing, and the weary fowls dropped the cumbersome troll at too high a speed. Ludicra was forced to hit the ground running, then she did a somersault and got tangled up in the ropes, vines, and trusses. Birds flopped helplessly to the ground all around her.

Gnat came next, because he was the lightest and had almost caught up to her. The gnome landed gracefully, already wriggling out of his harness. Filbum, Crawfleece, and Weevil landed in quick succession, and there were so many birds that the three of them began to put up a squawk. While the others untied the ropes and harnesses, freeing the fliers, Ludicra scanned the sky for a sign of Captain Chomp.

"He was right behind me," said Weevil. "Well, maybe *way* behind me."

Clipper alighted on the ground near Ludicra and motioned toward the vibrant underbrush. "There is a footpath that way, and it will take you to Darlingvale, the village where they hold Rollo. As I warned you, he has until tomorrow night to live. As soon as the Kissing Moon rises above the trees, he'll be killed."

"How far away is it?" asked Ludicra. She scanned the treetops, hoping to see Chomp, but the big ogre was still somewhere behind them.

Before Clipper could answer, a long, exotic birdcall sounded in the forest, and the fairy crouched nervously. "Fairies," she whispered. "Elves are not far behind. The birds will try to distract them, but all of you must hide."

"But Chomp," said Ludicra with alarm.

The fairy darted into the overgrown bushes and was gone. Ludicra whirled around and saw Gnat, Filbum, and Crawfleece pick up their harnesses and dash for the trees. Only Weevil remained behind, surveying the sky for Chomp.

A green bird zipped past them, making the troll and ogre duck. "Run, you dummies!" hissed Kendo as he circled overhead. "Don't let the elves see you!"

With that, the enchanted bird soared into the forest, and they heard shouts, muffled by the trees. *Elven shouts,* thought Ludicra with alarm. She grabbed Weevil and dragged the tall ogre into the vines. They flopped onto their bellies just as a squad of elves rushed into the clearing, their bows leveled for action.

From the sky came squawks and cries, and Ludicra craned her neck upward, expecting to see Captain Chomp surrounded by trouble. But no—it was just a skirmish between the fairies and the birds, who were swarming and swooping at each other like warring bees.

There came a low roll of thunder, and a warm downpour fell from the sky. Because they were hidden under the trees, the rain barely reached the trolls, ogres, and lone gnome. They squirmed deeper into the layer of loam on the forest floor, but the elves were caught in the deluge. They headed toward Ludicra's position, crossing the clearing in large strides for such short beings. Even the birds and fairies escaped from the rain, but that didn't help Ludicra.

Beside her, Weevil tensed and lifted her club, ready to do battle with the approaching enemy. It seemed as if they would be discovered with the elves' next step.

From nowhere, a huge figure swept over the trees and careened into the clearing. The elves barely had time to throw up their arms for protection as the monstrous shape smashed into them. With a loud grunt, Captain Chomp landed belly-first on three unlucky elves, and the rest were knocked aside like so many bowling pins. Exhausted birds, including two giant condors, also flopped on top of the elves, and all of them became entangled in the ropes and vines.

It was pure bedlam in the rainy marsh. One elf tried to draw an arrow, but his bow had been broken at the tip. When Weevil came charging from the brush, swinging her club, half of the elves ran in terror. The other half were already unconscious from Chomp's having fallen on them. Weevil drew a knife and quickly cut the big ogre out of his ropes, with the birds flapping all around. Ludicra ran out to help Chomp to his feet, and he looked around groggily.

"Did I land all right?" asked the ogre. "It felt a little bumpy."

"You landed great," answered the troll, "And now you've got to run great." Chomp nodded, but his thick legs were still wobbling, and so was his head. The birds looked too tired to fly as they scurried into the woods, jumping from branch to branch.

Ludicra spotted Crawfleece, Filbum, and Gnat waving to them from the underbrush. With Weevil's help, she dragged the big ogre to the tree line, where all helped to carry him. While the rain pounded down, the band from Bonespittle retreated noisily into the unfamiliar Bonny Woods.

High up in a nearby tree, the laughter was drowned out by a peal of thunder. "What a rich performance!" crowed Stygius Rex as he wiped his eye with a black handkerchief. He shifted to make himself more comfortable on the tree bough. "I haven't laughed so hard since the other mages ate my home cooking."

"And where are they now?" asked Clipper innocently. The fairy already knew the answer, but she delighted in her master's gleeful evilness.

He shrugged it off. "Some intestinal problem claimed them, curse their hides. But I will say that Bonespittle has been much drearier without them."

"And with *you* as the only sorcerer," added the demented fairy with a giggle. She looked around at the dripping leaves and branches. "I must say, the rain was a nice touch."

"That spell was easy to cast here," said Stygius Rex with satisfaction. "My elemental powers seem stronger on this side of the chasm. But, Clipper, we're going to a lot of trouble to do this—are you sure it will pay off?"

"Yes, master," said Clipper with a snicker. "When this band of trolls and ogres escapes—or appears to escape—I am sure the fairies and elves will attack Bonespittle. The fairies can fly, the elves can cross at the bottom, and they have catapults. After this attack, you can rally everyone in Bonespittle around your leadership. And the need to invade the Bonny Woods in turn."

The fairy clapped her delicate white hands and wiggled her wings. "Not only that, but I'll get back into Rollo's good graces."

"Watch that troll," said Stygius Rex darkly. "He always brings trouble."

"Not if we use the snake knife on him," whispered Clipper. She trembled with anticipation.

The wizard lifted a bushy gray eyebrow growing in a field of brown warts. "I see," he replied thoughtfully. "Then I get an ally who is popular with *everyone*. He can endorse me, or I could set him up as a puppet and work behind the scenes. Good thinking, my little henchfairy."

Suspiciously, the mage touched the black knife on his belt. "But I'll keep this . . . for now. I also keep the option of making sure that Rollo and his friends never return."

"As you wish, master," said the fairy, backing away. With a flutter of her wings, she was gone.

The battered band slogged through the strange forest, drenched by the downpour, lost, and afraid. Weevil and Crawfleece were in the lead, with Ludicra and Filbum helping the groggy Captain Chomp, while Gnat struggled to bring up the rear. Mostly they feared the elves' poison arrows. Ludicra still had half a skin of antidote to the poison, but she knew that was only enough for one of them.

They couldn't keep running headlong into the forest, and Chomp was going to have to rest and get his wits back. She wasn't sure it was a smart idea, but Ludicra finally called, "Halt! Everyone . . . Stop!"

With great relief, Ludicra and Filbum gently lowered Chomp to the ground, where the big ogre curled up and began to snore. Gnat eagerly caught up to them, and Weevil and Crawfleece marched back to their position.

"Why stop?" asked Crawfleece.

"Do you even know which way you're going?" demanded Ludicra. "Are we headed toward Rollo or away from him?"

The big troll shrugged. "Okay, I only know I'm going away from the elves."

"That's not good enough," said Ludicra. "Clipper showed me a path that she said would lead us to Rollo. He's being held prisoner outdoors, and that's good for us."

"Do you have a plan to free him?" asked Weevil.

"Well, we, uh . . . we have to see the situation first," answered Ludicra. "But I thought we could use our flying troll." She looked hopefully at Filbum.

The youth gaped at his comrades and stammered, "Oh, yes, sure . . . I can fly in and out and . . . do things." He blinked helplessly at Ludicra.

"We plan later," declared the troll. "Right now we've got to get back to that clearing and find the path to Darlingvale."

"The woods are crawling with elves," said Weevil. "We need a scout to go ahead—someone who won't be spotted easily." All eyes drifted to the smallest of their party, Gnat.

"All right," said the gnome. "I'll signal you with a bat squeak if I run into any elves. Should we go back along the path we just made?"

Ludicra squinted into the dark treetops, still damp with moisture from the unexpected shower. The forest seemed quiet and gloomy after the rain—even somber—but Ludicra knew that the peace was just an illusion.

"I wouldn't go that way," offered a cackling voice.

They all whirled around, unsure where the sound had come from. "Lower your weapons, please," said the annoying voice. "It's me, Kendo."

"Oh, the bird," muttered Weevil, lowering her cudgel.

"We owe the birds a great deal," said Ludicra, although Kendo made her nervous. "Come down, we won't harm you."

They looked up at the branches, but the parrot wasn't there. Instead he waddled out from under a low-slung fern. "You're lucky that we avians are keeping the fairies busy," snapped the colorful bird, "or they would find you for certain. The elves you can avoid, because so many of them are gathered in Darlingvale. Don't worry, I'll help you get there."

"We can't move until Chomp is better," said Weevil, pointing to the sleeping ogre.

"If we have some time," said Ludicra, "I would like you to hear a story that Kendo told me while we were flying. Will you tell my friends? I could do it, but you tell it so well."

The bird stuck his crimson chest out and began to preen his tail feathers. "Yes, most stories I can tell better than anyone else. I can't believe that no one in Bonespittle knows about the old Troll King, the missing treasure, the sorcerer Batmole, and why the Great Chasm was created."

"Tell us!" said Filbum, flopping to the ground in front of the bird.

So Kendo told them, in loving detail, the same way he

had told Ludicra. They gaped in awe at the bird as he revealed how the chasm had been ripped into the earth to separate the warring lands, and how the treasure had been stolen from the old Troll King. Then came the part about the angry sorcerer who didn't get paid, prompting all the sorcerers to take over Bonespittle and enslave the trolls.

Hearing it again, Ludicra was still mesmerized. Gaping holes in their history had been filled with moonlight, and the band from Bonespittle stared at the cocky bird. When he was finished, they sat in stunned silence for several moments.

"We're still in the middle of this story," said the bird, "even though it began a thousand years ago. The elves are still looking for the treasure, the two lands are still warring, and the trolls want their king back."

A voice behind them bellowed, "And what are you birds getting out of all of this?" All turned to see Captain Chomp, sitting up and looking alert.

"We're getting our vengeance too," declared the parrot. "We're just like the downtrodden trolls, except elves are worse than ogres—pardon the present company. That's because the elves like to eat us, and the fairies take all the good roosts and steal our eggs. This war has been brewing for a long time, and if Stygius Rex can help us—"

"Stygius Rex?" asked Ludicra puzzledly. "He's dead— he can't help you."

The parrot coughed nervously. "I meant . . . that he helped us before . . . on his first visit. He's the one who convinced the birds that we could fight them and win—with *my* translation, of course. It's a pity that he's gone, but he's still an inspiration. When I say 'Stygius Rex,' naturally I refer to all of our friends from Bonespittle."

The bird hopped across the ground and onto a branch. "If you're all awake now, why don't we take a roundabout route to the village. The gnome should still go ahead of the main party, so I can relay messages down to him. He can wave his hat to guide you—just keep him in sight. Are we ready?"

Kendo didn't wait for an answer; the bird simply flapped his large wings and cruised to a distant branch. Little Gnat hurried to keep up with him, while the others picked up their gear and trudged onward.

Ludicra felt a big presence loom near her, and she turned to see Captain Chomp. "Do you think we can trust that green jabberwock?" asked the ogre.

"I don't know," admitted Ludicra. "He seems awfully fond of Stygius Rex, and he talked as if the mage were still alive."

Chomp chuckled. "Well, he is like Rollo to the birds. He led them in a revolt against the powers that be in this accursed place."

"I suppose," answered Ludicra thoughtfully. "All of this gets confusing, doesn't it? Stygius Rex is their hero, and they're helping *us*. And how are we going to get back home . . . after we rescue Rollo?"

"I'll stay here the rest of my days," vowed Chomp, "before I let those birds fly me again." The big ogre shuddered, making the thick folds of his pelt jiggle. "So how are we getting home? *You* tell *me,* you're the leader."

"Thanks for the vote of confidence," said Ludicra, knowing that the decision did rest with her. This loyal band had followed her into the vastness of the Great Chasm and flown with the birds, so they would probably follow her to their death. They were in enemy territory, surrounded by the foe, and their only allies were a flock of birds and an undead fairy. With every step toward their goal, the dangers seemed to grow, and success looked more unlikely than ever.

"The bird and the gnome are moving fast," said Weevil. "Everyone, step up the pace!"

Ludicra looked around and realized that she was at the very end of the file, so she caught up with the rest. There was no point in letting them see how nervous she was, because they were all already wide-eyed and wary. The fun of the tunnel had been replaced by the terror of a woods full of elves, fairies, and poison arrows.

"I tell you, they have a flying ogre!" wailed a frightened elf after he staggered into the village of Darlingvale. "He's as big as a house! By himself, he defeated our whole force!"

Rollo was pretending to be asleep as he hung from the pillory; his head and arms were encased in wooden stocks, forcing him to stand. The troll was weary, sore, and thirsty from being exposed to the weather and the elves' scorn, but he hadn't lost hope. He was certain he'd have another chance to escape, although he couldn't have guessed it would involve a flying ogre.

From his position in the central square, the troll could hear much of what happened in the village. He listened intently to learn more, but Prince Thatch hurried the messenger into a hut. Suddenly Rollo felt a dirt clod hit him in the side, and he twisted his head to see a dark-haired elf snarling at him.

"Do you have more friends in our land?" demanded the elf. "Speak, you ugly troll!" His tormentor picked up another dirt clod and hurled it, hitting Rollo in the shoulder.

The young troll winced, then he grinned. "Ah, the army of flying ogres has finally arrived! They drop from the sky—look out!"

The elf cowered and stared upward, giving Rollo a welcome laugh.

Seeing his mirth, the guard spat at him. "We'll have our way with you, ugly troll! When the Kissing Moon rises, you'll get what you deserve." Sniffing haughtily, the elf returned to his post about twenty feet away.

Rollo closed his eyes and tried to look defeated, but he was thrilled at the news about ogres in the Bonny Woods. It had to be somebody he knew.

The leafy canopy of the Bonny Woods was so thick that it didn't seem as if they were traveling by day, thought Ludicra. It was more like a strange twilight, lit by fluttering slivers of sun that slipped through the leaves. The smells were still sweet and flowery, so unlike the dank odors of the swamp, and Ludicra was almost overwhelmed. For a while, she held her snout.

The hardy band was making good time, even if they often had to wait while Kendo and Gnat scouted ahead. Eventually Gnat's lamp-hat would wave above the thick underbrush, and they would march in that direction. In this way, the band made progress though the lush forest, even if they could see no path. Ludicra worried that they could easily be tricked by Kendo and the birds, but what would be the point? If the avians wished them harm, they could have merely left them alone in this bizarre place.

Ludicra felt it before she saw it—a strange vibration that shook the ground, causing a few water drops to cascade from the trees. Everyone in the band stopped to look around, and the vibration jarred the land again, shaking more old raindrops from the branches above. Every two seconds brought another shuddering of the earth, only now they also heard the snaps and crunches of trees breaking.

"Something is coming our way," muttered Filbum. Crawfleece quickly wrapped a protective arm around the smaller troll. "It sounds big!"

"An earthshaker?" asked Captain Chomp with a loud gulp.

"I never heard one that was so regular," answered Weevil as the forest trembled again and tree trunks snapped in the distance. "Where's Gnat?" asked the lanky ogre.

They all peered into the distance, but the gnome had disappeared into the underbrush, which only confirmed the approach of danger. With the next rocking of the forest, Ludicra staggered on her feet.

Captain Chomp looked around and grimaced. "It seems familiar somehow—"

Suddenly the ground shook with an overpowering force, knocking all of them off their feet. A huge tree trunk crashed to the forest floor, adding to the terror and confusion, and everyone in the party burrowed for cover. Ludicra cowered behind a clump of vines, thinking that the whole woods was about to fall into splinters. The climax came when the air was shattered by an enormous, reeking blast of air; it was the biggest burp the young troll had ever heard.

"He's back!" wailed Captain Chomp.

CHAPTER 12

AN OLD ACQUAINTANCE

"WHO'S BACK?" ASKED LUDICRA.

Before any of her comrades could answer, a huge shape flew over them and landed in the trees, crushing a great swath of the forest as it did. This was no elf or fairy—it was like a flying hill! After it cut loose with another monstrous eruption, the behemoth bounded off again, landing at a distance but with enough force to shake the Bonny Woods all over again.

"What was *that?*" asked Ludicra, poking her shaggy head out of the vines.

Filbum scurried toward Captain Chomp and asked, "Was he alone?"

"I don't know," croaked the big ogre, gazing fearfully at the treetops. "I always wondered what happened to that beast."

"What beast?" demanded Ludicra.

The others stared at her in amazement. "You never saw him before?" asked Chomp. "That was Old Belch, Stygius Rex's favorite mount. As foul as he is big." The others nodded in agreement.

"I couldn't even see it," said Ludicra with amazement. "Did you?"

"No, but we could *hear* him," answered Filbum with a shudder. "And smell him. There is only one beast that jumps like that—the giant toad." As if to emphasize his point, the ground shook with another tremendous landing somewhere else in the woods.

"Or is this *another* giant toad?" suggested Weevil.

"You would think there would be more than one," agreed Crawfleece.

While they discussed this theory, Ludicra gazed around at the overgrown forest. *Great, now I need to worry that we will be stampeded by giant toads.* "Where is Gnat?" she asked. "And the bird?"

Weevil pointed into the trees. "I think they went that direction."

"No, it was more that way," countered Crawfleece, pointing in the opposite direction.

While the ground periodically shuddered, Ludicra searched for Gnat's tiny footprints. Soon the others joined her, but the ground was so overgrown and filled with woodsy debris that they found nothing.

"Should we yell for them?" asked Crawfleece.

"No," whispered Ludicra, "we don't know who is out there." She looked around nervously and found the entire party gazing at her, waiting for a decision.

"Spread out," said the troll wearily. "Go in different directions and find Gnat and Kendo. I'll stay here . . . at this clearing we trampled. Don't go far, and use good judgment."

"Aye," said Captain Chomp forcefully. He glanced at the others, making sure they understood the orders.

The four searchers—two trolls and two ogres—each chose a direction and slunk off into the forest. Within a matter of seconds, they had disappeared into the lush undergrowth. Ludicra felt terribly alone. Nothing sounded in the damp forest but the chirping of insects and the gentle plop of raindrops. It was as if all life were hiding from the sizable terror of Old Belch.

As she stood in the forest, listening to the gentle lull of the insects, the troll's legs became very tired. She began to wobble on her feet, but she felt relaxed at the same time. With a gasp of surprise, she slumped onto the ground, still awake yet having lost the snap in her muscles. Yet Ludicra wasn't overly worried, because the buzz of the insects was oddly reassuring.

Without being told, she suddenly knew that her comrades were not going to return. She was all alone in this strange grove, surrounded by gentle sounds and great peace. The young troll couldn't even remember what had frightened her—all she could remember was Rollo's simple face and big sloping shoulders. She felt closer to him somehow, even though she wasn't doing anything to *get* closer to him. But for some reason, sitting in the middle of this enchanted glade seemed to be the perfect course of action.

The gentle breeze brought a smell of flowers, but almost too intense to be flowers. While Ludicra tried to guess the source of the sweet odor, she fell asleep and keeled over into the fallen leaves and twigs of the forest.

When the young troll maiden awoke, she found herself surrounded by water on every side, yet she wasn't wet. Instead the roaring liquid flowed straight down into a bottomless pit—right below a narrow ledge on which her feet wobbled. *I'm in the middle of a waterfall!* thought Ludicra with alarm. The troll shifted her bulk nervously until she felt the spray of cold water on her backside. She was in a dim grotto surrounded by rock walls that rose out of sight, and the only light came from a distant speck.

Her earth senses told her that she was underground, yet *above* ground . . . perhaps inside a mountain. *If this is a real waterfall, then that's a real drop beneath me!* thought Ludicra. *If I try to smash through the torrent, I'll probably fall to my death. And I still won't know how to get out of here.*

How did I get here, anyway?

"Chomp!" she called out. "Crawfleece! Can anyone hear me?"

Only the roar of the water answered her calls, but she still yelled until she was hoarse. Her cries were ignored by the rushing falls, which thundered inside the dark grotto.

Ludicra sunk down onto her haunches and covered her eyes. It was all the troll could do to keep from weeping in desperation, and she gulped back a sob. *I've failed! Rollo will be killed!* she thought miserably. *Fie, we'll probably* all *be killed. I've doomed Rollo and everyone in the party!*

As she bowed her bushy head in despair, Ludicra heard a melodious voice lifting above the crashing water. "Fear not, child," said the soothing tones, "because we mean you no harm. We only wish to see if you mean *us* harm."

Ludicra lifted her head and looked around at the walls of water surrounding her. The voice had seemed to come from everywhere at once—or else from inside her head. The young troll rose bravely to her feet and shouted, "We truly mean you no harm, although we will fight when attacked. We came only to save Rollo. Do you know Rollo?"

"Yes, I know Rollo," answered a weary voice. "I trusted him once, but I'm uncertain now. Do you know what has happened to the fairy named Clipper?"

"We just saw her," answered the troll. "She enlisted the birds to fly us from the bottom of the chasm. She's Rollo's friend, you know."

"Or so we thought," said the voice sharply. "This news only troubles me more, because we'd feared that Clipper would aid our enemies—in these days, that means the birds. I suspect that you and your band are being used for ill purpose."

"I don't know anything about your war with the birds!" insisted Ludicra. "I just want to find Rollo and save him before these savage elves kill him!"

"You call the *elves* savage?" asked the voice in amazement. "After *you* invade *us?*"

"They shoot us with poison arrows, place traps to maim us, and try to kill us at every turn!" answered Ludicra indignantly. "Would you say that's civilized? Where I come from, we've got swamp suckers friendlier than elves!"

"They're afraid," muttered the voice sheepishly.

"Pah!" snorted Ludicra. "They're not too afraid to invade us. Do you know that we found a large band of treacherous elves in *our* tunnels, on the Bonespittle side? They were treasure-seekers, and we drove them out—so that count is settled! Three of us invaded your land, and you sent *twenty* into Bonespittle."

The voice was silent for a long time after that. Finally it asked, "Did you kill these elves you found in Bonespittle?"

"We tried, but only got a couple of them," muttered Ludicra, then her brutish expression softened. "One of them was named Dwayne—he had golden hair and blue eyes. I judged him to be kind, and he saved my comrade's life."

"You had talks with them?" asked the voice.

"I told you I did!" snapped Ludicra. "Now show yourself. Or are you one of those cowardly elves who skulk in the bushes with a poison arrow?"

The troll was stunned when the waterfall completely evaporated before her eyes, leaving her standing in a dry cave, with no pit beneath her. She had to kneel to the ground and touch the cold stone before she could fully accept it. The roar of the water was gone too, and all she saw was a dusty cave with a rugged ceiling and a distant torch giving poor light.

From the shadows of the cavern stepped a slim figure dressed in flowing white. She was too large to be a fairy, and she had no wings—but the wizened creature seemed as ethereal as any of the fey folk. As the white-garbed stranger approached, Ludicra realized that she was a very old elven female. Despite her small stature, she had the bearing of a queen, and Ludicra could only hope that one day she would carry herself with such poise.

The elder regarded the troll and frowned. "Actually, I *am* one of those elves who skulk in the bushes. But I don't wield arrows, I wield spells. My name is Melinda, and they call me the Enchantress Mother."

"I don't care about you or me," declared Ludicra. "All I'm worried about is Rollo. You can't kill him—Bonespittle *needs* him! I think the Bonny Woods needs him too."

The Enchantress Mother smiled. "And what about yourself, child? Don't you need Rollo as well?"

Ludicra bowed her head, scrunching her flabby face in reflection. "I thought I deserved to have Rollo . . . and deserved to be queen of Bonespittle. But then I met

Dwayne. Even with all his soft hair and cuddly features, he's still attractive to me."

Melinda nodded in sympathy. "Ah, yes . . . Dwayne. He is cute, I'll grant you that. I approved Dwayne and his band's crossing the Great Chasm; I also approved using the black knife on Clipper. So I still have much to learn myself. What you are going through is called 'growing up.'"

"What about Rollo?" asked Ludicra, pleading with her outstretched claws. "I don't care about me, but Rollo must be saved."

The Enchantress Mother pursed her lips and wrung her delicate hands. "I fear that we are both playing into the wishes of others, and I don't know what to do about it. If Clipper is alive and in possession of the black blade, I fear that Stygius Rex is also alive. By aiding you, I may help them and destroy my own people."

"If you stand against Stygius Rex, then we are your greatest allies!" vowed Ludicra, snorting in excitement. "He may be dead or alive—or undead; it doesn't matter if we don't have Rollo. If we don't have our hero, we can't defeat the mage, because we can't rally the citizens. If you let Rollo die, then you are doing Stygius Rex a great favor."

"I wish you hadn't told me that," muttered the Enchantress Mother. "You make a good case, but first I must talk to one of your allies."

"Who's that?" asked Ludicra, looking around the dingy cave. "Where is the rest of my party?"

Melinda turned away, muttering, "I had to save them. They would have been killed otherwise."

"What do you mean?" growled Ludicra, knowing that she sounded like Captain Chomp, but not caring.

"Now don't be angry, but you were right about the poison arrows," said Melinda. "A band of our warriors were chasing the big toad, and they would have found you in a second. I put you all to sleep, so as to allow you to be captured. In return, they gave two of the prisoners to me."

"You captured *all* of us?" asked Ludicra in anger and surprise.

"No, I put you to sleep—*they* captured you," said Melinda with a sigh. "It was that or let them ambush you."

"Now we're really doomed!" yelled Ludicra. "You cheerful, happy elves will be the death of us!"

"You have not failed yet, child. Let me fetch my other prisoner." The elder elf brushed a slender arm clad in filmy white in front of Ludicra's eyes, and chanted softly, "Stay calm, if you will, and stand very still. If you can't be seen, you may yet be queen."

Ludicra felt as if she could still move, but she didn't want to. For whatever reason—magic or trust—she felt compelled to trust the old elf. However, she was still in despair about all of them being captured. *How can we save Rollo now?*

"This will only take a moment," said Melinda, padding off into the darkness.

While she was gone, Ludicra peered around the dusty, dry cavern, looking for a means of escape. This place was so different from the wet, drippy caves of Bonespittle—and she again felt they were at high elevation. She hadn't noticed it before, but there was a crack at the very top of the uneven ceiling, and Ludicra could see a handful of stars in the nethersky.

It's night! she thought with alarm. *We've lost a whole day. Rollo is supposed to die tomorrow!*

A loud squawk jarred Ludicra out of her worries, and she turned to see the Enchantress Mother stagger into view with a heavy cage in her hands. Inside the cage was the green bird, Kendo, gazing blissfully at the drab, dusty cave.

"Oh, do I get to live in all this splendor?" asked the bird in amazement. "With all these pillows and fruit baskets and salty fish bones? I must be in feathered heaven!"

"You are, Kendo," the Enchantress Mother assured him. Ludicra realized that the bird was seeing another of Melinda's illusions, much different from the one she had seen.

The elder elf went on, "We have wronged you so terribly that we want to make it up to you. And to all the birds. Tell me what we can do to make peace with you."

The big parrot fanned his crimson wing feathers. "First you must get the elves to stop eating us. That is just rude—little better than the behavior of those repugnant ogres and trolls."

"But I thought you were helping them," said Melinda

soothingly. When Ludicra started to protest, the elder held up her hand to silence her.

"We only helped them to irritate all of you," sniffed the parrot, "and to bring about your surrender. As I was saying, the elves must become vegetarians—and no caged birds, either! If we choose to live in your houses, then you can enjoy our company. Birds must be equal citizens, free to roost anywhere we want!"

"I agree," replied the Enchantress Mother. "These terms we can meet, but what about your friends? Helping a few trolls and ogres is harmless, but Stygius Rex and Clipper are not harmless. They're dangerous."

Kendo snorted a laugh. "Clipper is at least bearable now. As for the sorcerer, he united us. I don't think Stygius Rex would ever mean us harm."

"Would he leave the Bonny Woods if you asked him?" said Melinda.

"Oh, yes," answered Kendo smugly. "We're quite close."

The slender elf glanced at Ludicra and gave a slight nod. "Where is Stygius Rex now?"

"I don't know," cawed the bird. "Hey, why all this talk about *him?* Let me at some of those sunflower seeds!"

Kendo tried to move toward the illusion, but he bumped against the bars of the cage. With a squawk, the parrot realized that he was imprisoned. The Enchantress Mother swayed on her feet, as if her strength was ebbing. Ludicra ran from her frozen pose and caught the elder just before she dropped to the floor of the cave.

The irate bird called Ludicra every curse word he knew, but the troll ignored him as she placed Melinda in the dirt. Then she whirled on Kendo and snapped, "Have you ever seen a troll eat a bird? We don't cook you like the elves, we use our snouts to—"

"Never mind!" cried the parrot. "What is it you want from me? What will you take to let me go?"

"My comrades," she answered. "And Rollo." Ludicra looked worriedly at the Enchantress Mother, who was totally unconscious and breathing very lightly. She seemed to be in some kind of heavy trance . . . or maybe dying.

"Listen, bird," said Ludicra, rising to her feet. "The Mother Enchantress was telling the truth—Stygius Rex is not someone you can trust. When he takes over the Bonny Woods, it will be a wasteland, and you'll be slaves. You'll have his troops here too, and an ogre can eat more birds in one sitting than an elf can in a lifetime."

The bird gulped and covered his head with his wing. "I beg forgiveness. How can I redeem myself?"

"Do you know the way out of here?" asked Ludicra.

"Yes. Set me free, and I will lead you to the nearest opening." The bird glanced at the crevice high above them.

"No thank you," answered Ludicra, picking up his cage. "We'll both walk out. You'll have to earn my trust."

The big troll stomped into the shadows, carrying the container with the forlorn parrot inside. She noticed footprints in some rubble, and climbed over it to find a narrow crevice. With sheer determination, the troll squeezed her bulk through the crack, then she squished the cage to get it through. The bird squawked and complained, but she only gave it a dirty look.

A cool night wind struck her face, and she found herself on a ledge in the middle of one of the tors that dotted the Bonny Woods. If there was a way down—other than jumping—she couldn't see it. Even though she had lost the daylight hours, it was reassuring to see the darkness and the twinkling stars. Ludicra felt certain she could travel undetected with the night in her favor. The daylight was always too . . . suspicious.

"What are you going to do now?" asked Kendo smugly.

Ludicra glared at the treacherous bird. "Are you sure that Stygius Rex is alive? You've seen him?"

"Like I'm seeing you now," muttered the bird. "Not very pretty but as real as heartache."

"What do you know about heartaches?" asked Ludicra warily.

"A lot," answered the parrot. "That's what got me enchanted—when I fell in love with a snowy egret. Only I was a fairy at the time. After the council turned me into a bird, she wouldn't have anything to do with me! Who wouldn't know about heartache after a tragedy like that?"

Ludicra frowned at the green bird, but she still couldn't muster much sympathy. Instead she reached into his cage and grabbed him by the legs, then hauled him out and thrust him toward the stars. "Okay, fly then!" she ordered. "Get us down to the ground."

"Are you crazy?" cawed the bird.

To prove she meant what she said, the troll leaped off the ledge and went sailing toward the trees. The big parrot screeched and began to pump his wings furiously, which slowed them down only a little. But more important, the bird steered them between various branches until they could safely plow into a thicket of vines. The troll and the bird landed in a heap, with Ludicra clutching the parrot to her chest.

He clawed and pecked at her, trying to get away, but after all the adventures in the tunnel Ludicra had gotten fast at grabbing rope from her pack. She tied his feet together and wrapped the rest of the coil around his wings, so that he couldn't fly. Trussed up like a stuffed slug, Kendo was easy to sling over her back. Ludicra agreed with the Enchantress Mother—this was one valuable bird.

"You trolls *are* worse than the elves!" complained Kendo, twisting against her hairy back in futility.

"Quiet now," she cautioned. "Your fate is tied to mine. The elves and fairies consider both of us enemies, and I'll bet they would love to get their hands on *you*. It's simple— you tell me how to get to Darlingvale, where Rollo is held, and I will free you. That is all I require. It's all I've wanted from anyone on this quest."

Hanging upside down, the parrot nodded meekly. "Go toward that big palm tree. You will find a path. I will lead you there, but you had best be true to your word—or a million avians will be after you."

"Get me to Rollo," grumbled the troll, her bloodshot eyes blazing. *I've got a date to be queen,* she thought, but somehow it didn't seem as important as it had before.

CHAPTER 13
THE WOODWORKS

T HE DAWN SUNLIGHT STOLE ACROSS THE CENTRAL COURT- yard of Darlingvale, leaping into the eyes of the greasy troll locked in the stocks. His fur was matted down with eggs and rotten vegetables, and there were more lumps than usual on his big shoulders and back. Rollo looked up groggily from his fitful sleep and squinted into the intrusion. Only a few days ago, he had liked sunlight, now every dawn brought him a day closer to his death.

Tonight, when the moon rises, I will sink, decided the glum troll. He looked at the straw bales that the elves had piled up behind him—to stop any misguided arrows during their target practice, Rollo knew. *And I'm the target,* he thought miserably.

Rollo looked around and saw only a handful of guards

in the early daylight, but more were probably watching him from the huts. Ever since his failed escape and his imprisonment in this pillory, he had been helpless. The elves took turns heaping scorn and rocks at him, and he was never alone. Even now, the guards glanced suspiciously at him as they trudged across the square with their arrows notched in their bowstrings. The archers also scanned the sky, looking for birds or flying ogres from Bonespittle.

That's when Rollo heard it—the brutish growl of an enraged ogre! There was no mistaking that sound, because he had heard it so many times before. In fact, it sounded just like Captain Chomp. The troll and the elves all scanned the treetops, expecting to see a flying ogre wreak vengeance from the sky. Instead a large gang of elves staggered into the square, dragging a net full of angry ogre behind them. Rollo's heart sank, because he recognized that bristling lump of fur and tusks—it *was* Captain Chomp!

More weary elves entered the village, dragging trolls and ogres, all of whom were trussed up in nets and ropes. *My rescue party,* thought Rollo glumly. *They've all been captured.*

Upon seeing Rollo encased in the stocks, Captain Chomp grew quiet. So did all the other captured ogres and trolls, who were dragged into a pile in the center of the square. Rollo thought he saw one small bundle squirming in the nets, and he was shocked to think they had also captured a gnome. How had this brave band gotten across the Great Chasm?

"Let them go!" Rollo shouted to his captors. "They

haven't done anything. Your quarrel is with *me!*"

From the clutch of elves, one with a red beard strode toward Rollo. "Our quarrel is with all of you foul folk!" snapped Prince Thatch. "We will punish all who invade our land to attack us."

"Hey, big wad!" croaked a voice, which Rollo recognized as that of his sister, Crawfleece. "What about the elves who invade Bonespittle? What should we do with them, huh?"

Prince Thatch whirled on the captured troll. He was about to say something nasty, then thought better of it. This was the first Rollo had heard about elves crossing over to Bonespittle, and it only made him more confused.

"We aren't barbarians," said Prince Thatch with a friendly smile. "Rollo is the only one we're going to punish. The rest of you will watch and then report back to Bonespittle. I want all of you vile creatures to understand that we don't want you here, burning up the woods, wrecking villages, and bringing dead fairies back to life."

"How will you get us back to Bonespittle?" shouted Crawfleece. Rollo was surprised at how much he'd missed her nagging.

Prince Thatch puffed his skinny chest proudly. "We have a giant catapult we're building. According to our experts, it will shoot heavy weights across the Great Chasm."

"Getting ready to invade us, are you?" demanded Captain Chomp.

The red-haired elf snorted in disdain and turned to his underlings. "See that the prisoners have water . . . and a little food. And tell the workers to finish that catapult."

"Rollo!" screeched Crawfleece. "Are you all right? What have they done to you?"

"Pretty much as you see," answered the big troll with a shrug. "They've kept me prisoner for a week. They treated me well at first, until we resurrected Clipper and she flew off with the serpent knife."

"We've seen Clipper!" shouted Crawfleece. "She helped us to get here."

Now every eye in the village was on the bound troll lying in the dirt. Prince Thatch walked over to Crawfleece and demanded, "Tell me what you know about Clipper. Where did you see her?"

"Set us free," answered Crawfleece, "then I'll tell you all about the fairy."

"Pah!" answered the elf. "If she helped *you,* then we know which side she's on. And it isn't *ours.*"

"Then don't free us," answered Captain Chomp. "Kill us, but let us stand on our feet and defend ourselves."

"Hey, speak for yourself!" shouted Filbum. The small troll looked pleadingly at Prince Thatch. "Not all of us want to die, or even be here," he said. "Show me some mercy, and I'll tell you all about Clipper. And I'll go back to Bonespittle right now!"

Rollo wondered if his little friend was serious. Filbum used to be a coward, but the fact that he was here in the Bonny Woods, trying to rescue Rollo, made him seem pretty brave. More than likely, Filbum was up to something.

Prince Thatch stepped toward the squirming captive even as Filbum's comrades glared at the youth. Curled up in the dirt, bound hand and foot, the bedraggled troll didn't look very dangerous. "Cut this one loose," said the prince.

Rollo said nothing, because he was still in shock at seeing his sister and his friends in the same trouble he was. He couldn't blame Filbum for trying to save himself, but the other trolls and ogres looked very mad at their sidekick.

As the elves cut Filbum loose, the small troll asked, "What did you do with the other member of our party? The troll called Ludicra."

Now Rollo's bat-shaped ears perked up. *Ludicra had been with them? Why?*

"Have you hurt Ludicra?" yelled Rollo. "If you have, I'll . . . I'll hunt you down to the bottom of the bog pit! I'll mash your bones into glue! I'll pull out your nose hairs one by one!"

"Quiet," answered Prince Thatch with amusement. "I don't think you'll be doing any bone mashing, and it's none of your business what we do with our prisoners. She is safe . . . as safe as any of you."

Released from his bindings, Filbum staggered to his feet

and looked around. He rubbed his wrists and ankles where the ropes had dug in, then he glanced at Rollo and gave him a wink. The glum troll in the stocks tried to calm himself, but it was difficult. Rollo knew he had endangered the lives of his sister and his friends, even Ludicra, and it was all because he was selfish. *If I hadn't come back to the Bonny Woods, all of us would be safe and happy in Bonespittle.*

Prince Thatch glared at Filbum. "All right, tell me about the fairy."

"Well, she's about a foot tall, all dressed in white, with lovely wings—"

"I know that!" snapped the elf. "Tell me something about Clipper that I don't know."

Filbum scrunched his rubbery face in thought for a moment. "I know she followed us here, and I see her watching us."

"Where?" asked the elf in alarm, as he and his fellows dropped into combat stances.

"Right there!" Filbum pointed into the trees behind Rollo, and all the elves lifted their bows and aimed in that direction. Because his head was stuck in the stocks, Rollo couldn't follow their gaze, so he was the only one watching Filbum when the dumpy troll suddenly lifted off the ground. He was flying!

Filbum didn't fly fast, but it was easy to escape with no one watching him. Before the worried elves could turn around, Filbum had vanished into the trees. Rollo laughed so hard that tears sprang to his eyes.

"Where did he go?" thundered Prince Thatch. "Where is that foul troll?"

When no one could answer, the leader of the elves turned to Rollo, who was still chuckling. "You! *You* did this?"

"*I* did it?" asked Rollo in amazement. "I can't even scratch my snout."

"What about *you?*" demanded Thatch, staring at the other captives squirming in their bindings and nets. They grew very quiet indeed, although Rollo heard Weevil snickering.

The red-bearded elf waved his hands at his underlings. "Spread out! Find him." When they all started to run off into the woods, he corrected himself. "Wait! Those who live here in Darlingvale, stay and watch our prisoners. If anyone else escapes, you'll face the same fate as the troll."

Shaken by the sudden disappearance of Filbum, the other elves muttered among themselves as they wandered off. *Surely they know it was their own prince who had ordered him cut loose,* thought Rollo, *and maybe they'll have second thoughts about the rest of his orders.* He wondered again what they had done with Ludicra.

"Prince Thatch!" called Rollo. "In this fair land, doesn't a condemned troll get a last request?"

The elf scratched his pointy red beard. "I don't know . . . we haven't had a condemned troll in recent memory. It would have to be something very minor—and we're *not* going to set you free."

As Rollo spoke again, his voice cracked with emotion. "I would like to see Ludicra again. We were betrothed . . . to be married."

"Trolls get married?" asked the elf, shaking his head in wonderment. "We don't have much time, but I'll see if it's possible." He motioned two of his underlings to come forward, and then whispered orders to them. They dashed off into the woods.

Rollo slumped in his pillory, his entrapped limbs growing heavy. Still, they weren't as heavy as his doleful heart.

"Hey, Brother!" called Crawfleece.

Rollo lifted his head out of the stocks. His voice was a croak as he asked, "Yes, Sister?"

"Do you really want to make a hovel with Ludicra?" Crawfleece's snout wrinkled as she spoke.

"Yes," he rasped. "In a heartbeat."

Prince Thatch laughed. "Too bad, troll, that you're going to be target practice instead." He looked at his fellow elves, who appeared spent after hauling the heavy invaders into Darlingvale. They watched the sky and the forest nervously, for they had not bargained for disappearing trolls and flying ogres.

Filbum flew as far as he could into the forest, but he was no sparrow. In moments, he was smashing into boughs and getting tangled in hanging vines, and a branch slapped him in the face. With a thud, the dumpy troll crashed to the forest floor, but he quickly picked himself up, shook off the leaves, and began to run. If there was one thing Filbum was good at, it was running from trouble.

He hoped his friends didn't hold it against him that he had escaped. He hoped even more that he would figure out a way to save them, even if the situation did look hopeless.

The troll ran pell-mell, never looking behind him and hardly looking in front. The only place he looked was at the ground, to avoid tripping over vines and logs. Branches continued to slap him in the face, and vines still tried to grab him. With his eyes on the ground, he kept running until suddenly a big hairy log swung from the trees, taking out his legs. Now Filbum tumbled head over heels and landed flat on his back, knocking the breath out of his lungs. He gasped for air as something huge and hairy landed on top of him.

"Ssshhh!" hissed a voice.

"Ugh . . . urg . . . argh," he wheezed in a strangled croak.

"Ssshhh!"

His eyes were screwed tightly shut from fright, so Filbum couldn't see his attacker. He felt the creature roll off his pinned body, grab his leg, and drag him at high speed. Suddenly the two of them dropped into a hole, and he felt his body oozing into a pool of mud. That was a comforting feeling, and Filbum managed to open his eyes a crack.

He saw Ludicra holding a talon to her blue lips, warning him to be quiet. Then she pulled a pile of dried brush over their heads, camouflaging them in their muddy hole. A moment later, the troll knew why they had to be quiet, as a number of grumbling elves tromped past their position.

The pair of trolls waited until a parrot cawed somewhere high in the trees, then Ludicra lifted the brush and stuck her head out. "You did a good job of getting away," she said with a smile. "And you really *can* fly."

"I told you so," answered Filbum proudly, "and when I'm scared, I go like a dragonfly." Then he blinked at her and asked, "Were you watching us?"

Ludicra nodded. "I had just climbed up a tree to get a better view of the village when they dragged you in. Kendo and I were watching you. Rollo—is he all right?"

"No one from Bonespittle is all right in this crazy place," said Filbum. "Is Kendo with you?"

The female troll rolled her eyes and nodded, as a bright green parrot fluttered down to a nearby branch. "Have I fulfilled my end of the bargain?" asked the bird imperiously.

"Yes," said Ludicra. "You brought me to Rollo. You're free to go, but stay away from Stygius Rex and Clipper. They don't want to help you—only themselves. If they take over the Bonny Woods, it won't be a better place."

The avian nodded thoughtfully. "Maybe you're right. The war has brought us pride, but also misery. Our nests and eggs have been destroyed, and we have no time to sing or play. But what about you? How will you rescue your band?"

Ludicra shrugged her beefy shoulders. "I don't know.

We're two trolls against hundreds of elves . . . and hundreds of poison arrows."

"Hmmmm," said the bird, cocking his plumed head. "I think I know something that may help you. Follow me, and keep low. I will warn you if there's any danger." With that, the bird flew to a distant branch and waved to them with an outstretched wing.

Ludicra and Filbum crawled out of the mud hole and followed the green avian. "Where are we going?" whispered Filbum.

"I don't know," admitted Ludicra. "But I'll look at anything that could help us."

Cautiously they stalked through the woods, avoiding the roving bands of grumbling elves. Ludicra decided that the fey folk didn't look very happy either; all this warfare and anxiety was taking a toll on them, too. Surely, everyone in the Bonny Woods just wanted to go back to the way things were before . . . before Stygius Rex ever reached his icy claw across the Great Chasm.

By midday, Ludicra and Filbum reached something she had only seen a few times in her life—a road. It looked broad and was rutted with the imprint of wheels, like the roads that went to the Fungus Meadows and the Rawchill River. They skirted to the side of the thoroughfare, keeping hidden in the lush cover of the brush and trees.

Cautiously Kendo led them to a large clearing, where there were wooden barns, stacks of lumber, coils of rope, rows of tools, and piles of rocks. There were also neatly stacked bales of grain and an empty corral. In the middle of this camp was a monster—a contraption of rope and wood, levers and wheels, with a huge wooden spoon in the middle. Thick twists of rope bulged from the beams like the muscles on Rollo's arms. The incredible device towered over the barns like a giant stork, or an avenging mace.

Filbum gazed at the empty corral and sighed. "It looks like there were ponies here."

"They're gone now," said Ludicra, walking toward the wooden monster. "These elves are fairly skilled with cross beams and knots, and they make straight notches. What do you call this thing, Kendo?"

"A catapult," answered the bird, alighting on the top of the great spoon. "I believe you turn this wheel and twist the ropes until you have enough tension, and that flings the scoop off the ground. I have seen them hurl rocks and even a bag of sand a good distance."

"Yes!" exclaimed Filbum excitedly. "That red-headed imp told us about his giant catapult. He said he could hurl us across the Great Chasm with this. What do you think, Ludicra?"

She turned toward the preening parrot. "Have the elves chosen to desert this place?"

169

"They haven't stayed here for several days—since the discovery of Rollo," Kendo answered.

"There's lots of hay," said Filbum hungrily. "At least we'll eat."

"We'll do more than that," vowed Ludicra, looking around the encampment. She spotted a ceramic bucket full of foul-smelling black tar. At least that's what it looked like, although this brew was even more pungent than the usual swamp tar. "What is this?" she asked.

"Pitch," answered the parrot. "They use it to seal the beams. Be careful, because it burns."

The young troll smiled, showing her impressive fangs. "It burns, does it? Kendo, you have to fetch some big birds to help us—those condors from the canyon would be good. Filbum and I will study this machine, and test it. It shouldn't be too hard for a troll to fathom."

"This lever releases the boom and hurls the rocks," observed Filbum. He pointed to a rod that pulled a rope attached to a sliding hook. "I figure that you can adjust the range with either the weight of the payload or the tension on the ropes."

With a grin, Ludicra patted Filbum on the back. "Hey, you actually paid attention to Master Krunkle's lessons in bridge building."

"But you never did," scoffed Filbum. "You were always too busy grooming your underarms."

"But I always had smart fellows like you around!"

Fondly Ludicra rubbed Filbum's knobby head, then turned toward the parrot, who was still sitting on the scoop. "Hurry, Kendo, we only have until nightfall! And bring us some rags . . . something that will burn."

"Tee-hee!" The bird chuckled. "This sounds like fun!"

CHAPTER 14

THE KISSING MOON

ROLLO SQUIRMED UNCOMFORTABLY IN HIS PILLORY, BECAUSE he could see the filament of a ghostly white moon creeping above the treetops. He wasn't the only one who saw it, as every elf stopped in his tracks and gazed at the sudden apparition. Then they looked back uneasily at him—whether he saw guilt or anxiety, the troll couldn't tell.

Chomp, Crawfleece, and the others from his rescue party lay trussed up tightly on the ground, able to do little but squirm and snarl. If they made too much noise, the archers threatened them with their poison arrows, which had a sobering affect. Torches twinkled in various corners of the village, and every elf was out of his hut, watching the young troll intently.

Rollo shivered at the sight of the moon's crest, and

Prince Thatch took note and began to laugh. "You have time, stupid troll, because we don't proceed until we see the moon's sweetheart. I was also waiting for word about your betrothed, to see if we could bring her here. No word yet. I'm trying to be a sympathetic host; however, these are troubled times. We'll wait a spell, but don't place much faith in that."

The prince turned to the gathered villagers and bowed low. "Elves of Darlingvale, thank you for coming to the first troll archery contest. Many of you were in my command when we found the prisoner, a troll named Rollo, guilty of crimes against our citizens. He invaded the Bonny Woods not once but *twice,* and he burned our forests and incited the birds to war against us."

The elf sniffed and motioned to the pile of ogres, a troll, and a gnome. "As you can see," Thatch continued, "he has brought more of the foul folk into our realm. But we are a compassionate race, so we will punish only the one who has struck against us twice. There will be no third time for Rollo to disturb us."

"What about elves who invade Bonespittle!" shouted Crawfleece. Rollo could only blink in wonder at his sister, because he knew nothing about that. And now she had mentioned it twice.

"Will you be quiet with that untruth?" snapped the red-haired elf. "I don't want to use you for a pincushion too, but I will."

"Quiet down, Crawfleece!" shouted Rollo, his voice barely a croak. "If this will bring us peace and save your lives, I'm ready to go."

"No!" shouted the ogres. "Release him! It's unfair!" Rollo heard their pleas, but the elves ignored them and went about their preparations. The condemned troll stared at the tip of the moon until his friends' voices died out. As the milky orb crept above the trees, Rollo tried to lift his head to make it appear lower—but his thick neck was fixed in the stocks. There was no way he could stop the moon from rising.

Prince Thatch crossed before his admirers, who were cheered by the idea that their trials were finally going to end. "Performing before you tonight," he announced, "shooting at our special target from two hundred feet, are the greatest archers in Darlingvale and the shire!"

There was fevered applause, and the beaming prince went on, "Plus I have invited the champions from my own royal guard—twice winners of the Bonny Woods Invitational." There was polite applause, and Rollo began to struggle in his bindings. His weary muscles screamed with pain as his struggles produced nothing but more raw sores under his fur.

"Let me introduce the archers!" intoned Prince Thatch with great flair. He strode toward a line of elves, all of whom possessed deadly long bows almost their own height. They were small but sinewy, and all had flinty eyes that bespoke confidence and experience. *At what part of my body will they take aim?* wondered Rollo. *And will I have to stay in these stocks?*

"Quarrelsly of Comelydale!" announced the prince, tapping the first stalwart on the shoulder. "Murphy of Fiefdom! And the Jackel Sisters!" The elf went on to name many more of the archers waiting to poke a hole in Rollo, and the sheer numbers made it seem that the contest would be short—at least from Rollo's point of view.

The troll was in a daze until he heard a huge burst of applause, and he looked up to see an elf taking position at some distance. Rollo tried to squeeze his body behind the stocks and posts of his pillory, but his head and limbs were still sticking out. The crowd fell into a hush of rapt attention.

"The Kissing Moon," whispered many voices, and Rollo managed to lift his head just enough to see the full moon brushing against a bright star. The two celestial bodies seemed to bask in each other's ghostly glow, and Rollo realized that this would be the last sight of his life.

The next instant, he heard the stinging whistle of an arrow as it sped toward him in the darkness. The prisoner caught his breath just as the arrow thudded into something hard. *Wood!* Rollo concluded with relief, because he didn't feel any worse.

That brought a gasp from the crowd and a mutter from the distant archer. Another one quickly took his place, and the crowd quieted again. Before the elf could unleash his missile, a *thunk* and a loud *whoosh* came from somewhere in the dark jungle; then a blazing chunk of fire arced in the night sky. The elves screamed as the missile plummeted into their village, smashing a hut into flaming embers.

Suddenly a black figure floated above the smoke and fiery carnage; it looked more like a giant bat than anything else Rollo had ever seen. The high-pitched voice that came from the apparition was vaguely familiar.

"I am Stygius Rex!" squawked the black thing as it bobbed in the air. "Foolish elves! Cut loose all of my subjects at once, or I will level this village. *At once,* do you hear me!"

Instead the elves cut loose with a shower of arrows, and the miniature Stygius Rex flew upward with blazing speed. Another fireball came streaking across the sky—not like the sorcerer's erratic bolts but another graceful, arcing rainbow of flame. It smashed into more huts and exploded like a ball of burning rags. This sent the rest of the elven spectators scattering for cover, and the archers had no idea where to shoot. It was chaos in Darlingvale!

Out of the flickering glow of the fire, a full-size figure dashed toward Rollo. This apparition crouched behind him and lifted a hammer and chisel to the chains that held the stocks in place. "Did you miss me?" whispered a soothing voice. "I'm still ticked at you for running away."

"Ludicra!" he gasped. Rollo nearly wept with joy, because she was alive and by his side! Somewhere the fake Stygius Rex was squawking at the elves, who were screaming and panicking while another fireball arced gracefully from the forest. It smashed into the roof of the pagoda, showering them all with burning debris.

"The chains are broken," whispered Ludicra. "Head toward the chasm. That way." The incredible troll pointed into the smoke.

"I'm not leaving your side," insisted Rollo. "Ever again."

With a grin, she threw off the top beam, and he was able to lift his arms and neck from the stock. Rollo's muscles screamed with pain and relief as she undid the chain from his ankles. Trying to muster some balance and strength, the troll staggered off the platform.

"How did you do all this?" he rasped, pointing to a burning hut.

"A catapult, run by Filbum and lots of birds. You don't look too sturdy—wait right here for a moment." Ludicra kissed him on the cheek and dashed into the firelit chaos.

With a happy sigh, Rollo staggered against a post. He tried to look smaller than he was, even though the elves were firing into the blazing embers swirling above the flames. Rollo was jostled by someone in the crowd, and he turned to see a red-bearded elf.

Prince Thatch's eyes grew as wide as the buttons on his vest; then he drew a short sword and vowed, "I'm going to skewer you myself!"

Bang! A hammer landed on his head, dropping the elf into a lump of forest-green flannel. Ludicra looked down at him and clucked. "This one is very annoying."

"Yes, he is," answered Rollo weakly. "Our comrades?"

"I've given them knives—they're cutting their way out. Come on!" His heroine grabbed his arm protectively and hustled him into the smoky chaos. With a fiery *whoosh,* another fireball streaked into Darlingvale, sending more sparks and citizens scattering.

It was all a blur to Rollo as they dashed between the flaming huts and lodges. The trolls knocked down elves as they ran, and the archers were unable to shoot because of the panicked villagers blundering into their line of vision. The pair of trolls bounded into the woods, with Rollo following his champion blindly. They heard others crashing through the brush behind them—a few sounded like their friends, but most were elves, hot on their trail.

The Kissing Moon was fully risen, giving off almost as much light as the sun, and Rollo realized they were on a path. "Where are we going?" he asked his wonderful rescuer.

"To the Great Chasm," she answered, panting from exhaustion.

"And then what?"

"I don't know," admitted Ludicra. "This is farther than I thought we would get."

"Wait up!" growled a voice, and they turned to see Chomp, Crawfleece, Weevil, and a gnome and ogre whom Rollo didn't recognize. They clasped arms and barked greetings over the din, but there was no time for a proper reunion—arrows were whistling through the leaves, danger-ously close.

"Keep moving!" ordered Ludicra. "Filbum will meet us farther along."

"No I won't!" squeaked a voice. "I'm here now!" The dumpy troll fell from the sky and rolled along the ground until he banged against a tree trunk. Then he looked grog-gily at Rollo. "How do you do the landings?"

"I'll tell you if I ever figure it out," said the bigger troll with a grin. He reached down and lifted his friend to his feet, as shrill elven voices rose above the commotion.

An arrow thudded into Weevil's shield, which she wore on her back. The lanky troll instantly picked up the gnome and charged down the footpath. "That's enough small talk," she said. "Now run!"

Rollo had a hard time keeping up, so weak and sore was he. Because they were on a trail, both the strangers and the locals were able to keep up a good pace, but the longer-legged trolls and ogres managed to put some distance between themselves and their pursuers. Weevil carried the gnome, Crawfleece hovered protectively over Filbum, and everyone helped each other as best they could. Still, a whistling arrow was never far behind them, and Rollo fig-ured that the elves were regrouping in numbers.

Captain Chomp jogged wearily beside Rollo, and the big ogre snorted. "Can't we just make a stand and wipe out a bunch of them?"

"Old friend," said Rollo, "you just stole me from death—don't make me go back so soon. You know they aren't the real foe—and you know who is. At the Great Chasm, I suppose we'll fight. . . . I don't know what else we can do."

"You can fly," suggested the ogre.

Rollo gulped. "I can barely walk at the moment, and I want to stay with my friends . . . and Ludicra. This calamity is all because I thought I was doing a good deed for Clipper!"

Chomp scowled and snorted. "Didn't your mother always warn you to stay away from good deeds?"

"Yes," admitted Rollo, hanging his woolly head.

"Well, listen to your mother," said Chomp, cuffing him on the back of his head. An arrow sunk into a nearby branch, and he pushed the young troll ahead of him. "Rest later—now run!"

As more arrows zinged through the darkness, the weary band stumbled down the footpath. A parrot cawed, and Ludicra waved them off the path into the jungle. Rollo followed the panicky file until he found himself climbing through slippery gravel and thorny weeds. They were in the foothills of a tor, thought Rollo, probably the big hill close to the rim of the chasm. That's where he had been caught in a spiderweb many days ago, and life hadn't gotten much easier since then.

He looked over at Ludicra and his allies, and he realized

that life had never been better. They had thought enough of his hairy hide to come all the way across the Great Chasm to rescue him. Bursting with pride, the young troll was about to thank his comrades when a shimmering bauble suddenly flitted in front of him. It hovered before his eyes until he was able to gradually focus on the delicate shape.

"Hello, Rollo. Remember me?" asked Clipper with a perfect midair curtsy.

The troll skidded to a stop, and Chomp bumped into him from behind. "What is it?" asked the ogre.

Rollo whirled around, but the ethereal creature was gone. The others in their band were charging up the tor, leaving Rollo and Chomp behind. Suddenly the troll and the ogre heard loud sneezing behind them, and they saw elven silhouettes among the trees. The enemy was awfully close at hand, though only the sneezing had given them away.

Someone grabbed Rollo's arm and yanked him around, and he saw Ludicra's puzzled face. "What is it?" she asked.

"Elves right behind us." Rollo grabbed her and pulled the plump troll into a crouch. "Clipper made them sneeze . . . to slow them down."

"Move it!" whispered Captain Chomp, pushing both of them up the hill. "I like the idea of getting to high ground."

In due time, they rejoined the others, and the band plodded up the foothills of the tor. Somewhere among the brambles and jagged rocks, they lost their pursuers and crawled under an overhang to rest.

"We should keep moving," urged the gnome. He glanced at Rollo and grinned, showing off his yellow teeth. "The name is Gnat. I'm Runt's nephew. I say we keep moving, because they're right behind us!"

"What are we going to do at the Great Chasm in the dark?" asked Ludicra. "We'll fall off the edge."

"For that matter, what are we going to do there by daylight?" wondered Weevil. The lanky ogre looked to Rollo, and soon everyone gazed at the bedraggled troll. He didn't know why he was their leader, because their feat of coming to his rescue was more heroic than anything he had done. Lately he'd done nothing but bungle badly and get himself captured.

"I know what!" squeaked a tiny voice. Everyone looked around, because the voice hadn't come from anyone in the group.

A sliver of moonlight seemed to fall from the trees, and it coalesced into the fairy, Clipper. Although she looked like the fey creature he had befriended on his first trip to the Bonny Woods, there was now a spark of mischief in her eye, and her air of innocence was gone.

"If you want to help," said Rollo, "why don't you bring me back my knife."

"It's not *your* knife," said the fairy haughtily. "I'm much in your debt for bringing me back, Rollo, but let's understand exactly who is in command. It's not me or you. The black serpent knife is a mage tool, it belongs in his hands . . . until we can safely get it away from him. But that's a subject for another night. Now we have to get this brave band to safety."

"The elves say you're evil," declared Ludicra.

"Oh, are you going to believe those nasty rumors?" asked Clipper, sounding hurt. "Didn't I get you up here? Didn't I do everything you asked?"

The fairy put her arms on her slim hips and darted into Ludicra's face. "Listen, you ninny, you know what treatment you'll get from the elves! They're dipping their arrows in poison right now. If it wasn't for me, you'd be dead already. I'll grant you this much—you surprised me with the way you rescued Rollo. I was ready to let the elves make him a dead hero. Now there's a good chance to get all of you home alive, if you'll do as I say. You're only a handful, so don't fight against an army of elves."

Rollo knew she was right, but he couldn't fully trust her. "Where is Stygius Rex?" he asked.

The fairy shrugged. "I don't really know. This is my first solo assignment, and I don't want to mess it up."

"I'm ready to go home!" offered Filbum.

"Another flying troll," said Clipper with a sly smile. "Impressive, but until you can fly over the Great Chasm, it's of little use to us. I have arrangements to make, and the birds are keeping the fairies busy. I doubt if they'll attack at night, so go ahead and stay here until dawn. Then come to the rim of the chasm—you'll have no trouble finding us."

"*Us?*" asked Rollo hesitantly.

"Just wish me luck," said the fairy before she flitted away.

Rollo looked wearily at his fellows. "What do you think we should do?"

"Bloodthirsty elves on one claw," said Weevil, "and a crazed sorcerer and his ghoulish fairy on the other." The haggard ogre shook her head. "Rollo, this is the same Stygius Rex you killed a few weeks ago, and he *might* be mad about it."

"I know one thing: I'm not flying with the birds again," vowed Captain Chomp, pounding his fist in the dirt. "I'll stand to fight . . . and buy you time."

"The elves found a way down to the bottom from this side," Filbum pointed out.

"Do you think the elves will give us time to look for it?" asked Captain Chomp. With a groan, the old warrior crawled from the shallow cave onto the outer ledge. Stiffly he rose to his feet and said, "Weevil, you're on first watch with me."

"Yes, Captain." Her bones and leather creaking, his old comrade crawled into the open. After a few words, the ogres ambled down the hill to take up hidden positions.

Without warning, Crawfleece reached over and shoved Ludicra into Rollo's chest, and he caught her comforting bulk in his arms. Blissfully the two of them cuddled together in the dark hollow, and so did Crawfleece and

Filbum. The others squirmed until they had made sleeping pits in the dust.

The third ogre shook Rollo awake. "Hurry . . . elves coming," insisted Motley.

"Okay." Rollo blinked his eyes and saw that it was still dark outside. He awoke Ludicra, who was curled in a large ball nearby, and the two of them helped Motley wake the others.

Quickly all the trolls and ogres stumbled onto the ledge, where the gnome was already on guard. "Hurry!" hissed Gnat. "They found our trail." As if in confirmation, an arrow clattered at Rollo's feet.

Ludicra was quickly in the lead, and Rollo fell in line behind her. As they skidded down the tor in the opposite direction, Rollo could see that it wasn't the dead of the night at all, but almost dawn. The sky was slate-gray to the east and getting a pinkish tinge around the edges. With any luck, they would be at the rim by full light, although Rollo still didn't know what they would do there. Trusting Clipper was a terrible risk, but they didn't have many choices.

Upon reaching level ground, they dove back into the overgrown forest. At every step, vines tried to trip them and branches slapped them. When Rollo fell, Ludicra helped him up, and he returned the favor a moment later. Gnat plunged ahead of them and found another path; it looked familiar to Rollo, but at this point everything was a sea of thorny green. He longed to get back to the simple mud of Bonespittle, and he wondered, *Why did I ever seek adventure?*

It seemed as if the band ran for hours, trusting Gnat and Ludicra, who had the best sense of direction. The ogres protected their backs with their shields, which was a good idea with all the arrows slicing through the forest. As the sun rose higher and the light improved, the arrows increased in number. Motley took one in the rump but didn't tell anyone—he kept running until he suddenly dropped dead from the poison. There was no time to mourn for the fallen ogre, and his comrades simply picked up his shield and fled.

"Oooh, I want to fight them!" growled Chomp, shaking a fist at the cowardly archers, who fired from cover in the leafy underbrush.

"I'm sure you'll get your chance!" yelled Crawfleece, charging past them. "Where is that fickle fairy? She's supposed to help us!"

"The rim of the chasm!" shouted Gnat from the front.

Carefully they broke from the forest onto a sandy strip of land that hugged the cliff as if it feared to fall off. There were plenty of escape routes from this point, but they were all straight down into the misty depths of the canyon. If they expected to see birds or steps to help them, there were none—just the gigantic, gaping maw of the gorge.

Rollo tried not to look down, because he felt too weak to fly. Plus he wasn't going to leave his comrades again. Behind them, he could hear the elves shouting orders as they began to venture from the woods. They were getting ready to attack the exposed band.

"Clipper!" yelled Ludicra. She waved her comrades to follow along the deadly rim, trying to keep moving. "Fairy, show yourself!"

Suddenly the ground trembled with a resounding shudder, followed by a deafening burp and a blast of air so putrid it reminded Rollo of home. They stared in the direction of the eruption and were again staggered by the shaking ground. Even the chattering of the elves behind them had stopped.

Old Belch, the sorcerer's giant toad, bounded toward them along the rim of the canyon. Herding the monstrous amphibian was little Clipper, who pushed futilely at the toad's rear end when he didn't jump quickly enough. With one final spring, the toad landed right in front of them, and they gaped at its monstrous sliminess and broad back, which would easily carry all of them. He waddled around until his bumpy head was pointed across the chasm.

"Can he make it across?" asked Filbum worriedly.

"He has a better chance than any of *us*," answered Weevil.

Clipper hovered over their heads. "Hey, you don't have time to think about it! They're taking aim!"

Rollo whirled around to see the elves oozing from the forest, forming ranks of archers along the rim, getting ready to send a deadly volley in their direction. "All aboard!" he shouted.

Every troll, ogre, and gnome among them clambered onto the toad's greasy back, an imposition that he hardly seemed to notice. They grabbed warts, pits, and handholds in the grimy folds of his flesh, and he shifted a little. The fairy zoomed over them, nodding with satisfaction.

If Clipper wants to get rid of us, this is a good chance, thought Rollo worriedly. But he didn't think Old Belch would sacrifice himself for such a plan. He hadn't gotten old by being that foolish. Suddenly the toad turned his head and ripped loose with a monstrous burp that knocked over the first two lines of elven archers. Some of them tumbled into the chasm, and others scrambled to safety. Still others dashed out of the forest to take their places.

"Let's go, if we're going!" shouted Captain Chomp.

Clipper seemed to agree, as she shot a stream of fairy dust at the grumpy toad. At once, the amphibian sunk down as if gathering himself for the effort. His massive muscles rippled under his rough exterior, and Rollo could feel a primal energy filling the rarefied air of the Great Chasm. Even the elves stopped what they were doing to watch an event that they would tell their grandchildren about for generations to come.

Sitting beside the Troll King, Ludicra, Chomp, and everyone else tensed in the same fashion, waiting for the wild ride that was destined to take place. Rollo thought he heard Clipper cackling softly, but he looked around and couldn't see the fairy.

The toad suddenly swelled up as if taking a great inhalation of breath, then every muscle rippled in the same direction at the same time. Incredibly long and powerful hind legs launched the bulk of the beast into the air, and it sailed off the rim, arcing across the misty canyon. Rollo wasn't sure if he himself was screaming or not, but many of his comrades were howling for their lives.

As the wind tussled them, Ludicra clutched Rollo's pelt with one claw; with the other she grasped a crusty wart on the toad. "You know," she said, "you don't have to marry me. I just wanted you to be safe."

He laughed nervously and tried not to look down. "I'm not sure I would call this *safe!*"

Ludicra laughed too, and Rollo put his arm around her. "Whatever happens, I won't feel safe without you," he rasped.

They peered into the wind, but there was nothing to see but the blue sky and the back of the toad. Gradually they soared downward, past the crest of the jump, and Rollo watched them dip below the level of the Bonespittle side. As the jagged cliff loomed closer, the young troll stared with alarm.

We're not going to make it to the other side!

All of them screamed: four trolls, two ogres. and a gnome named Gnat. Who wouldn't scream if they went plunging into a bottomless canyon on the back of a toad? They had started out wanting to go across, and now they were just going straight down. The only one laughing was Clipper, who dove like a feathery spear right beside them.

As they hurtled downward, screaming and clutching each other, Old Belch flattened himself into a saucer. Great flaps of skin branched out from the toad's stomach, and he caught a thermal air current and glided upward. Rollo's stomach flipped at the sudden change of direction, but he shouted with delight along with everyone else.

Now they were sailing through the canyon, and although it was clear that they had dropped too far to get to the other side, they could survive this gradual plunge. Everyone breathed easier, and Rollo and Ludicra reluctantly let go of each other.

A black cloud passed over them, and Rollo looked up to see a big bird—or some flying creature—vanish over the canyon wall into Bonespittle. "Did you see that?" he asked Ludicra.

"What?" she shouted.

"Never mind!" The wind made it too loud to talk, and there was much to see on the way down. Great strata of rock etched the sides of the gorge, revealing countless layers of history. Still, the deeper they went, the more shadowy and darker it became, until the only light was the gash of blazing red far below them.

"There's a snake on fire down there!" Rollo shouted in alarm.

"That's not a snake," Ludicra answered with a laugh. "It's the river of lava from the volcano!"

Rollo put his snout close to Ludicra's floppy ear, which she didn't seem to mind. "You've been down here before?"

"Oh, yes," she answered. "And there's a way up to Bonespittle. But we have to get the toad to land on the right side!"

Even seen in dim twilight, the bottom of the canyon was impressive, with its burning rivers, great black boulders, and nasty plant life. At one point they flew above what looked like people scampering over the rocks, and everyone shouted at once as they spotted these elusive figures.

"The fiendish elves!" shouted Gnat.

Most of the fey folk ducked for cover, but a few elves paused to stare at the giant toad as it sailed past them. One even shot a pointless arrow at the beast, missing them by many lengths.

"Are those the elves who invaded Bonespittle?" asked Rollo. As they neared the bottom, the wind wasn't so fierce, and they could hear each other.

"Yes," answered Ludicra, sounding embarrassed. "They're looking for treasure down here." She blinked at him, flashing her long hairy eyelashes. "Oh, you don't know about the old Troll King and the sorcerer named Batmole. And the deal they made . . . and the treasure that got lost somewhere down here?"

"No!" said Rollo excitedly. "There really was an old Troll King? Tell me about it, please."

So she did, telling him about the elemental wizard, Batmole, who was hired to create the Great Chasm with eruptions and floods. How he never got paid, because the Troll King's treasure was stolen, and that led the sorcerers to take over Bonespittle, throwing out the Troll King and enslaving the trolls. "And ever since," she concluded, "the elves have been looking for the treasure."

"It's all true!" said Rollo in amazement. "All my father's crazy stories—"

"Coming in for a landing!" bellowed Captain Chomp.

Rollo peered over the flapping skin of Old Belch and saw with relief that they seemed to be on the Bonespittle side. The river of lava gave the gorge an eerie red glow, making it look like the Dismal Swamp during the Leech Festival.

Banking back and forth, Old Belch zoomed in for a landing. It looked like a good angle to Rollo, but the mammoth toad plopped down with a bone-shattering thud that set off a dozen geysers and made the earth tremble. All of the passengers were thrown off the toad's back to land in tiny thuds all around him. With a howl Crawfleece came to rest in a small pool of lava, and jumped to her feet with her clothes on fire. She scooted her rump along the ground until the flames went out.

Clipper hovered over the crash site, and the fairy gazed

at them with mischief. "You're a sorry lot, tee-hee. Don't worry, you just have to find the stairs and you're as good as home! I'll keep those elves away from you!" With a cackle, she darted off.

"We made it!" cried Filbum, waving his arms. "We rescued Rollo, and we're ready to go home as heroes!"

"And Rollo will be the king he deserves to be," said Ludicra, squeezing his arm happily, although she sounded a little sad that the adventure was over. Rollo knew how she felt, because even though they seemed safe, there were still things to worry about.

"Those elves," grumbled Chomp, smashing a beefy fist into his palm. "I wish we could take care of them before we go."

"Oh, let the fairy do it," said Weevil. "She seems to get such a pleasure out of bedeviling them. And we *should* be proud—we accomplished our mission."

"What about the treasure?" asked Gnat slyly, looking at Rollo. "That does belong to the trolls . . . and the Troll King."

"There's no such thing as a Troll King until we get home and have a coronation," insisted Crawfleece. "And you're not allowed to run away this time, Brother."

"I won't," promised Rollo with a grateful smile. "But what about Stygius Rex?"

"He stayed in the Bonny Woods, didn't he?" asked Filbum. "That's what the bird said."

Rollo glanced around at the twisted, overgrown plants and glowing red river. "Let the elves search for the treasure," he said. "They've been looking for thousands of years, so a little longer won't matter. We've got to go home and find out what's happened to our families and our villages."

Before he marched off, Rollo stopped to gaze at the dirty, bedraggled band of trolls, ogres, and the lone gnome. "I just want to thank all of you . . . my comrades," he said, his voice cracking. "I never dreamed you would go all the way across the Great Chasm to rescue me. Then you fought elves and fairies, and poison arrows. You're the best friends a troll ever had!"

"You got that right!" answered Filbum, as everyone joined in the laughter.

"Most trolls don't even have any friends!" added Chomp. "But you have many, including one spectacular friend. She kept driving us and never gave up—you would be a pincushion without her. That's your future queen, Ludicra. Without her, no way do I fly up this canyon hanging from a bird!"

"I see," said Rollo, putting his arm around the young female troll who had rescued him. He remembered how he had used to tag along after her, afraid to even say hello. Ludicra's baby fat had been melted off by her ordeal, and her jowls weren't as pudgy as they used to be—but she looked more stunning than ever. "If we have a king, then we should have a queen," he announced.

A cheer went up, with Crawfleece's voice yelling the loudest. "Come on," yelled Rollo's sister, "let's get our king and queen home before anything else happens to them!"

Then, putting their brawny arms around one another's hairy shoulders, the members of the weary band marched off into the red glow of the Great Chasm.

ABOUT THE AUTHOR

JOHN VORNHOLT HAS HAD SEVERAL WRITING AND PERFORMING careers, ranging from being a stuntman in the movies to writing animated cartoons. After spending fifteen years as a freelance journalist, John turned to book publishing in 1989. Drawing upon the goodwill generated by an earlier nonfiction book he had written, John secured a contract to write *Masks,* number seven in the *Star Trek: The Next Generation*™ book series.

Masks was the first of the numbered *Next Generation* books to make the *New York Times* best-seller list and was reprinted three times in the first month. John has seen several of his *Star Trek*™ books make the *Times* best-seller list. Since then, he has written more than fifty books for both adults and children.

Theatrical rights for his fantasy novel about Aesop, *The Fabulist,* have been sold to David Spencer and Stephen Witkin in New York. They're in the process of adapting it as a Broadway musical. John currently lives with his wife and two children in Tucson, Arizona. Please visit his Web site at: www.vornholt.net.

Visit The Troll King trilogy Web site: www.troll-king.com.